# THE SACRED DIARY
# OF ADRIAN PLASS,
# CHRISTIAN SPEAKER, AGED 45³/₄

## Books by Adrian Plass

# ADRIAN PLASS

## THE SACRED DIARY
## OF ADRIAN PLASS,
## CHRISTIAN SPEAKER, AGED 45³/₄

**ZONDERVAN™**

GRAND RAPIDS, MICHIGAN 49530 USA

ZONDERVAN

*The Sacred Diary of Adrian Plass, Christian Speaker, Aged 45³/₄*
Copyright © 1996 by Adrian Plass
Illustrations copyright © 1996 by Dan Donovan

First published in Great Britain in 1996 by HarperCollins*Publishers*.
This edition published in 2005 by Zondervan.

Requests for information should be addressed to:

Zondervan, *Grand Rapids, Michigan* 49530

Adrian Plass and Dan Donovan assert the moral right to be identified as the author and illustrator of this work.

ISBN  978-0-310-26913-7

A catalogue record for this book is available from the British Library.

Any Internet addresses (websites, blogs, etc.) and telephone numbers printed in this book are offered as a resource. They are not intended in any way to be or imply an endorsement by Zondervan, nor does Zondervan vouch for the content of these sites and numbers for the life of this book.

*Interior design by Nancy Wilson*

*Printed in the United States of America*

*This book is dedicated to Jeremy Gates*

# ADRIAN PLASS

## THE SACRED DIARY
## OF ADRIAN PLASS,
## CHRISTIAN SPEAKER, AGED 45³/₄

# DIARY – A. PLASS

## Monday 31 Jan

Got a bit distracted in church during the message yesterday. Very clever visiting speaker. So clever that I hadn't got the faintest idea what he was talking about.

Suddenly said very loudly near the beginning of his talk, 'Who will stand and declare the Lord's displeasure with churches that are unrepentantly cleistogamic?'

Richard Cook, who was sitting next to me, leapt to his feet and said, 'Indeed, Lord, we rebuke and we stand against those cleistogamic tendencies that exist in our church!'

When he sat down I leaned over and whispered in his ear, 'What does cleistogamic mean?'

He whispered back, 'I don't know.'

Honestly!

Decided, as the talk droned on, to start up a diary again, just for a while, so that I can record some of my experiences connected with being a Christian speaker. Lots of invitations for the next three months, and as I have to use up oceans of leave before the end of the financial year, I'll be able to do quite a lot of them.

Unbelievable the way it's all taken off. Started with being invited by local churches to read bits from what I'd written, but over the last couple of years I've been all over the country. I do speak a bit as well as doing the readings now. Anne says it sounds all right when the things I say are true, but that when they're not I sound like a pompous git – I think that's the expression she used. Her ministry of encouragement is subtle and special.

Seems hardly possible that my three books about people in our church have been read by so many people. Glad Gerald persuaded me to send my first diary off to a publisher, although it was a bit of a shock to find what was supposed to be a serious, helpful account of daily Christian living, being described by critics as a 'searing satire on the modern church'. Slightly galling also to find some of my important personal spiritual insights being labelled as 'ludicrous modern religious attitudes, hilariously caricatured'.

Still, if they say it's searing satire I suppose it might be. At least I've mastered the process now – all I have to do is write seriously and everyone laughs their heads off. Really hope this book will end up being used as a sort of serious textbook for Christian speakers, but after seeing what happened to the first one I wouldn't be surprised if it became regarded as a major influence in the field of begonia culture.

We shall see ...

Must look up 'cleistogamic' in the dictionary.

## Tuesday 1 Feb

Decided this morning that I ought to have one of those support groups that lots of other Christian speakers have. The more I pictured it the more I liked it. I would be God's chosen vehicle, powerful and mantled with authority in public, yet restrained and full of grace in private, opening myself up in humble submission to the ministrations, advice and criticism of a little group of folk who would feel privileged and proud to be part of what God was doing through me.

Mentioned the idea to Anne and Gerald over breakfast.

'The thing is,' I said, 'that I'd submit myself to their advice and criticism and be sort of accountable to them, and er ... that sort of thing.'

Anne stopped in mid-toast-buttering, did a little laugh, and said, 'But you absolutely *hate* criticism, darling. You always have done. You get very cross indeed when anyone says anything remotely critical – doesn't he, Gerald?'

'Mum's right, Dad,' said Gerald, 'criticism's one of the things that makes little bits of spit appear at the corners of your mouth.'

Absolutely appalled by this response to my idea. 'I do *not* hate criticism, Anne – I've never heard such rubbish in my life! How can you possibly say that? I have been given the heart of a servant.'

Gerald said, 'I don't think the transplant's taken, Dad.'

Ignored him.

'And I do not get "very cross". You make me sound like – like a toddler who's been told he can't have another sweet. I'll have you know that God has done a mighty work of building in me as far as the whole area of criticism's concerned. Frankly, you couldn't be more wrong if you tried.'

Both burst into laughter at this point, for reasons that totally escape me. Gerald so busy cackling he didn't realize the end of his hair had flopped into the marmalade. I was slightly consoled by this.

When she'd recovered, Anne said, 'I'm sorry, Adrian, I'm sure God has done a mighty work of building in you, it's just that –'

'It hasn't been unveiled yet.'

'No, Gerald, don't – that's not what I was going to say. What I was going to say,' Anne continued in her sensible voice, 'was that you *have* changed. You're quite right. You *are* much more aware of problems and faults in yourself that, in the past, you never even noticed. But, let's be honest, darling, you're still not very good at – well, hearing about them from other people, are you? There's something useful and rather splendid about telling big halls full of people that you're not a very good person, but you're completely in charge of what people are allowed to know about you in that sort of situation, aren't you? In fact, they think all the more of you for being so honest about your shortcomings, so, in a sense, you win all ways, don't you? And that's great, as long as you can also take a bit of criticism from people like us, who are close to you and aren't going to be quite so easily impressed.'

She reached over and took my hand. 'I'm sorry, darling. Gerald and I shouldn't have laughed at you like that just then. It was just so funny that you got very cross indeed when I criticized the fact that you get very cross indeed whenever you're criticized. Well, you did, didn't you? Adrian, you do see what I'm getting at, don't you?'

Paralysed temporarily by the battle raging inside me. Didn't want to appear sulky or angry because both were bound to be interpreted as failure to accept criticism, but didn't want to speak, knowing it would come out sounding sulky or angry because that's how I actually felt. Managed a sort of glassy-eyed, wooden nodding movement.

'If it's any use to you, Dad,' said Gerald, who'd been scribbling on the back of an envelope, 'here's a little verse on the subject:

> 'Freely I confess my sins,
> For God has poured his Grace in,
> But when another lists my faults,
> I want to smash his face in.

'Does that more or less sum it up?'

Couldn't help laughing. Anne made more coffee.

I said, 'So you don't think the support group idea is a good one?'

'Oh, yes,' said Anne, 'I think it's an excellent idea, as long as you're going to be genuinely vulnerable, and not just use it as a means of – well, emphasizing and relishing your "stardom". That's not what you want, is it?'

Made me sound like Liberace.

'Oh, no ... no, that would be awful. I'd hate that ...'

'You don't want to waste their time either, do you? Tell you what – why don't you ask Edwin to choose a group and set the whole thing up for you? He'll know the best people to ask.'

'Oh,' I said, 'I was rather thinking that I might choose who comes.'

'Exactly,' said Anne and Gerald in chorus.

Reluctantly but sincerely thanked God for my family before going to bed tonight.

Wonder if Norma Twill will be in my support group. Not for any particular reason really. Just wonder if she will because – well, because she's very er ... very nice.

12

## Wednesday 2 Feb

*2:00 p.m.*

Just had lunch at work with Everett Glander, who's still not converted after over ten years of contact with me – the great travelling evangelist!

Suffering a real attack of nerves. If I can't manage to convert the person who's been sitting next to me for a decade, how am I going to make an impact on anyone else? What *do* I think I'm doing? I mean, it's not as if I even feel like the sort of person you'd imagine God would use to communicate to people. And what makes me think a group of busy people are going to want to waste their time supporting me when they're all doing important things themselves? And why ever would God want me, of all people, to go and represent him anyway? Suppose he actually *doesn't* want me to represent him, but my ears have been stopped by Satan. What if the devil's got me wrapped round his little finger? Suppose I'm an active agent of evil without realizing it. What if I'm Antichrist? What if I *am* the Beast of Revelation, destined to be thrown into the lake of fire for all eternity?

Bit worrying, really.

*11:30 p.m.*

Showed Gerald what I wrote at work when he came in this evening. He read it and said, 'Yes, very balanced piece of thinking, as usual, Dad. You don't think you might have got just a tad carried away? When the angels are strolling slowly through the city of gold enjoying their Beast 'n' chips wrapped in old sheets of *Mission Praise,* I don't somehow think it'll be you they're consuming.'

Told him I didn't really believe what I'd written – just felt a bit silly assuming that God was 'sending me out', as it were. He nodded very thoughtfully, and said he'd give the matter careful consideration.

Don't know what's going on with Gerald at the moment. Not sure whether we should be worried about him or not. He's left his job and come back home to live. Lovely to have him here, but what's going on? Living on his savings at the moment, and says he's got a big decision to make. Anne and I keep finding ourselves hovering nervously behind him as if he's likely to explode at any moment. Keeps going off for long walks, or working for hours on his word processor or just spending time quietly in his room.

Says he'd like to come with me when I go to do my talks. That's a good sign – isn't it?

Surely.

## Thursday 3 Feb

Free day today to do some preparation.

Came down late to discover that Gerald had already gone off for one of his marathon strolls. Found an envelope on the kitchen table addressed simply to '666'. Very amusing, I don't think. Four sheets of paper inside. First one read as follows:

Dear Satan's Plaything,

Had a think about what you said yesterday, and came to the conclusion that you only need to begin worrying when you do start to feel that you're the kind of person God would be foolish not to use. He's always used idiots – sorry, I don't mean you're an idiot – you know what I mean. What I'm trying to say is, there aren't any special people, only ordinary ones. If he decides you're of some use, that's his problem, not yours. Thought you might be interested to read the enclosed rewrite of Scripture that I've been working on. Don't suppose it was really any different then. Ordinary people – that's all there is.

Love,
Son of the Beast.

14

Made myself a coffee, sat down at the kitchen table, and unfolded the three sheets of paper that had been in the envelope with the note. Have copied down Gerald's 'rewrite of Scripture' here. Wonder what God thinks about it? I have a funny feeling he probably bends the rules for Gerald ...

After these things the Lord appointed another seventy also and sent them two by two ahead of him to every town and place where he was about to go. He told them, 'The harvest is plentiful but the workers are few. Ask the Lord of the harvest, therefore, to send out workers into his harvest field. Go! I am sending you out like lambs among wolves. Take neither purse nor scrip, nor sandals; and do not greet anyone on the road.'

And behold one of the seventy raiseth his hand and enquireth, 'When thou sayest "sandals", Lord, do we taketh that to be an generic term which denoteth all forms of footwear, or focusseth thou in on sandals in particular? I asketh only because I possesseth an exceeding fine pair of walking boots, ideal for those who hiketh around as thou art indeed commanding us to do.'

Before the Lord could reply, another breaketh in and saith, 'Lord, I heareth what thou art saying, but behold, the skin that undergirdeth mine feet and also the feet of mine friend, Fidybus – he who maketh a pair with me as we getteth on well over long periods and always have done since we playeth together as children ... Er, the object of mine speech escapeth me ...'

Jesus saith wearily, 'Something about the skin that undergirdeth thine feet, and those of thine friend, Fidybus?'

'Ah, verily, yes, it cometh back now. The skin that undergirdeth mine feet is like unto that which undergirdeth the feet of mine friend, Fidybus, in that it very soon waxeth tender and painful on rough ground. And it just striketh us that the sight of two men who holdeth heavily on to each other and hobbleth slowly and painfully along, going "Oo!" and

"Ah!" and "Ow!" whensoever they putteth down a foot, might cause those who dwell in the towns and places to which thou sendest us to scoff when we imparteth the news that the Son of God approacheth presently. "What state musteth *his* feet be in, if he cannot keep up with these two clowns?" they will mock. Might, therefore, Master, we ask thine blessing on the idea of wrapping strips of rag round and round each of mine feet and each of those belonging to mine friend, Fidybus? After all, strips of rag falleth well outside the dictionary definition of sandals, dost thou not agree?'

And behold, an veritable babel of footwear-related queries filleth the air, and Jesus raiseth his hand and saith, 'Hold on a minute! Let me maketh myself clear. No sandals means nothing on thine feet, all right? Nothing! Neither walking boots, nor strips of rag, nor tennis shoes, nor high-heeled slingbacks, nor Wellingtons, nor roller-boots, nor skateboards, nor anything that I mighteth construe as an sandal in the broadest sense of the word. Understandeth thou all? Good. Now, departeth thou in twos and –'

'Er, excuse me, Lord.'

'Yes, Thomas?'

'Regarding thine command that we travel in twos.'

'Yes?'

'Er, no one desireth to go with Thribbiel.'

And the Lord enquireth, 'Well, why doth no one desire to go with Thribbiel? He looketh all right to me.'

'He's a bit funny, Lord.'

'Well, we're *all* a bit funny, aren't we? Anyway, I invariably organizeth it so that we have even numbers. Who goest thou with, Thomas?'

Thomas replieth mournfully, 'No one desireth to go with me either, Lord. No one picketh me even at junior school.'

'Well, for all thou knowest, Thribbiel might desire to accompany thee?'

'I doubt it.'

'Well, let's ask him, shall we? Thribbiel, dost thou wish to accompany Thomas?'

'Yeah, Lord, but canst thou ask of him that he cometh over a bit less negative? He can be an real Eeyore.'

'Thomas, canst thou do that?'

'I doubt it, but, verily, I will try.'

'Good,' saith the Lord, 'now, mayhap, we can get on. Departeth thou in twos and –'

'Command Thribbiel that he be less funny, Lord. There existeth little point in me being more positive if he maketh no attempt –'

'Sorteth it out between you!' saith the Lord. 'Verily, this whole affair beginneth to feel more like an Brownie picnic than an commission to establish the Kingdom of God.' He pauseth to collect himself. 'Now, I repeateth my command that thou departest in twos, take neither purse nor scrip nor sandals and do not greet anyone on the road. Now, go!'

But immediately one of the seventy raiseth his hand to ask of the Lord if an small pink face-towel mighteth be taken, and that setteth all the others off all over again. One enquireth concerning his personal toilet kit which fitteth nicely into an little pocket specially sewn into his robe by his mother, another pleadeth to be allowed an small stuffed animal without which he feeleth insecure at night, and yet another postulateth an situation in which he meeteth the Lord himself on the road, and querieth whether the command not to greet anyone applieth in that case, until, behold, there ariseth an great clamour of foolish enquiries.

Then the Lord shouteth for silence, and saith, 'Look, I don't think we've quite grasped the theory behind this trip, have we? The idea is not that thou smugglest sundry items into thine luggage using as an crummy excuse the fact that stuffed toys cometh not under the Oxford Dictionary definition of sandals, but rather that thou art dependent on me! Understandest thou that? No purse, no scrip, no sandals, no teddy bear, no Barclaycard – just go!'

Then an lengthy silence falleth, and just as Jesus believeth they are truly about to depart, an nervous hand raiseth itself.

Jesus regardeth the owner of the hand with narrowed eyes. 'Yes?'

'Er, regarding thy command that we should take no scrip, Lord?'

'Yes.'

'Well, er, to be honest, I knoweth not what an scrip is, Lord, and, well, it worrieth me that I might er, taketh an scrip without realizing I've got it. So I just thought . . .'

On hearing this the remaining sixty-nine scoffeth loudly, laughing, and crying, 'Hah! Thou dolt! Knoweth thou not what an scrip is? Surely all possesseth that knowledge. What an div!'

Then Jesus gritteth his teeth and saith, 'Very well, who can telleth us what an scrip is?'

Behold, the confidence of the sixty-nine draineth away. One hazardeth an guess that an scrip is 'what you use in an play'.

Jesus shaketh his head and saith, 'All right, how many knoweth not what an scrip is?'

All seventy raiseth their hands.

Jesus emitteth an little sigh, and smileth to himself, and saith, 'Okay, taketh the weight off thine feet. Behold, I commenceth from the beginning . . .'

## Friday 4 Feb

Much cheered and inspired by what Gerald had to say yesterday. He's absolutely right! I do qualify to speak for God because I am just an ordinary follower. Rather fancy I now have a greater appreciation of that fact than most. Really feel ablaze for the Lord! Can't wait for tomorrow's meeting at something called the 'Reginald and Eileen Afternoon Tea Club' in West Hammerton, one of our local villages. Those folk have specially requested me to come. They're looking forward to it, and I'm not going to let my stupid worries about myself spoil their enjoyment, or their access to things of the Lord.

Hallelujah!

## Saturday 5 Feb

Arrived at West Hammerton Village Hall with Gerald at two-thirty, well in time for my talk which was scheduled for three o'clock. Walked into the hall wearing my shy, yes-it's-me-folks-but-I'm-no-different-from-anyone-else expression. Needn't have bothered. No one seemed to know who I was.

Approached as we entered by a smartly dressed, very elderly man of stiffly military, but somewhat unsteady bearing, who introduced himself as Mr B. Granger, secretary of the Reginald and Eileen Afternoon Tea Club. Said the person who'd actually invited me wasn't able to be there because he was dead (a pathetically lame excuse, Gerald commented later), so he didn't really know what was going on.

Things were further complicated, he explained, in his age-muffled bark of a voice, by the fact that I was an alternative to someone who, as far as I was able to understand it, wasn't able to fill in for a man who couldn't take the place of a woman who'd backed out of substituting for some wonderful person called Mr A. Whittle, an expert on 'West Hammerton As It Was', who everyone had really wanted to come (with his slides) in the first place.

Did my talk involve slides?

No, it didn't.

Oh.

In response to a question from Gerald, Mr B. Granger explained that the Reginald and Eileen Afternoon Tea Club derived its name from the fact that it had been founded many years ago by two people called Reginald and Eileen, who were also dead.

Gerald nodded intelligently.

Most of the twenty or so elderly people sitting round little tables in groups of four or five glared at me as I followed Mr B. Granger to the place where there would have been a microphone if they'd had one.

They hate me, I thought, for not being Mr A. Whittle, and for having no slides.

Mr B. Granger glanced covertly at a small piece of paper in the hollow of his hand, and cleared his throat commandingly.

He said, 'Make a start, then, ladies and gentlemen. Notices first.' Pause. 'There are none. Any notices from any member before introduction of speaker?'

An ancient, white-haired little lady who was almost bent double, levered herself up from her chair and zig-zagged her way determinedly to the front, from which vantage point she addressed the assembly in quaveringly aggressive tones.

'I just want to say,' she announced, 'that I've been taking all six club tablecloths home and washing them once a year for the last twenty years, and I'm not prepared to go on doing it. It's time someone else had a turn.'

'What is involved, Mrs Lazenby?' enquired Mr B. Granger, in sternly official tones.

'You have to take all six tablecloths home once a year and wash them,' said Mrs Lazenby rather predictably. 'Only I've been doing it for twenty years, and I think I've done my bit. It's time someone else had a go. I'm not prepared to go on doing it. I've done it for twenty years, and I think that's long enough. Someone else can –'

'Mrs Lazenby has been doing it for twenty years,' interrupted Mr B. Granger, presumably realizing that the repetition of this complaint was affording Mrs Lazenby enormous satisfaction, and that she would probably go on making her point indefinitely if nobody stopped her, 'and I think she's done her bit. It's time for someone else to have a go, because she's not prepared to go on doing it.' He cleared his throat again. 'I should like to propose a vote of thanks to Mrs Lazenby in recognition of the work she has undertaken in relation to the club tablecloths over the last twenty years. Shall we express our appreciation in the usual way as she now steps down from the post in which she has so magnificently served for –'

'Twenty years,' filled in Mrs Lazenby with relish, 'and I'm not prepared to –'

'Perhaps a volunteer would present herself – or *him*self,' ripple of laughter, 'during the refreshment period immediately following the talk. Thank you once again, Mrs Lazenby, for your sterling endeavours on our behalf.'

Mrs Lazenby, accompanied by a patter of frankly grudging applause, reluctantly but triumphantly wove her way back to her table, where she immediately embarked on a fiercely whispered discussion with her two immediate neighbours about the fact that she had done it for twenty years and wasn't prepared to do it any longer . . .

'Now,' Mr B. Granger ticked off Notices on his little piece of paper, 'we come to our speaker. And we are indeed most fortunate to have secured the presence of Mr E. Bass, a much loved local lay reader.'

(The only things he got right were geography and sex, which, as Gerald said later, are not a lot of use unless you're an itinerant gynaecologist.)

'Mr Bass's talk, to which we are all looking forward to – er . . . with a great deal of pleasurable anticipation, is entitled –' quick squint at the piece of paper, 'it is entitled "Readings from *The Scared Dairy*", and will take us up to tea at twenty-five to four. There are no slides. Thank you, Mr Bass.'

The only person in that hall, not excluding myself, who enjoyed my slideless 'Readings from *The Scared Dairy*' was Gerald, who loved every minute, of course. The rest of my audience stared at me with either undisguised puzzlement or deaf incomprehension as, with my top lip sticking uncomfortably to my teeth, I agonized my way through half an hour of completely inappropriate material which failed to raise even the glimmer of a smile. It was like trying to water plants with sand.

Not helped by the fact that, about ten minutes before the talk ended, two ladies from different tables got up at precisely the same moment, as if by magic, and disappeared into the kitchen, where they spent the next ten minutes clattering and chinking and slamming things, and talking in voices loud enough for them to be able to hear each other speak over their own clattering, chinking, slamming noises.

Totally drained afterwards. Only one question from the floor when Mr B. Granger invited them.

Was I acquainted with a Mr A. Whittle, who spoke a commentary with most interesting slides of old West Hammerton? No, regrettably, I was not acquainted with Mr A. Whittle who spoke a commentary with most interesting slides of old West Hammerton.

This piece of information seemed to kill off any further interest. Felt a strong desire to kill off Mr A. Whittle, and send him, with his slides, to entertain Reginald and Eileen.

Needed my tea badly. Gerald was really good with the old folk. Got them laughing and chatting with ease. Wish he'd done the talk. I never want to do another one again – ever.

Meeting finished with the singing of the club song, led by a piano in the corner which seemed to be missing almost as many original ivories as the old gentleman who played it with wobbling panache. The words of the song, sung twice through with great gusto, went like this:

> Reginald and Eileen may not be with us now,
> For they, with many friends, have passed away,
> But sad though we may be, we will gather here for tea,
> And show the world that we are proudly gay.

Gerald drove us home. I sat miserably clutching my previously written Thank you card ('We all much appreciate the new insights into the work of our dairies that you have brought to us this afternoon') and my five-pound note, wondering how to cancel all further engagements. All the way back Gerald, who still seems to feel the need to tear the guts out of every joke, produced depressingly accurate impressions of Mr B. Granger saying, 'Mr E. Bass, a much loved local lay reader, whose talk is entitled "Readings from *The Scared Dairy*".'

Anne, and Thynn, who'd come round for tea, in hysterics when Gerald told them about my sepia photograph of an experience.

Perhaps my support group should be composed entirely of chronic depressives, then they could have a good laugh twice a month at my expense.

Poor old Leonard's still a bit shaky since the death of his mother. Still, as he said this evening, at least she'll be able to hear what all the heavenly beings are saying now. The thing that drove Leonard mad towards the end of her life, was that she refused to wear a hearing aid because, according to her, she wasn't deaf, she just couldn't hear what people were saying.

We see a lot of L.T. at the moment.

## Sunday 6 Feb

Had words with God in church today. Asked for something to lift my spirits about the whole speaking business. I seem to so easily lose confidence.

Looked up as I came out of church with the others and saw a cloud that was shaped just like South America. Idly wondered if this could be 'the sign'. Pointed the cloud out to Richard Cook.

I said, 'You see that cloud that's shaped just like South America? Do you think it could be a sign?'

He said, 'Yes, it could be, except that it isn't South America. It's shaped exactly like Italy. That's remarkable! God's calling you to Italy.'

Thought I'd better see what everyone else thought.

Gerald said he thought it was the continent of India.

Anne (who loves the West Country) said it was definitely the Lizard peninsula in Cornwall.

George Farmer knew it was Greenland, which, he said, confirmed something he'd always thought about me.

Thynn said it was a carrot, and suggested that I was being called to minister among those who labour among root vegetables.

Decided it wasn't the sign I was looking for, not unless God is expecting me to convert most of the planet, *and* people who labour among root vegetables. I mean, God created the world, didn't he? So he must be able to draw one little bit of it accurately if he wants to.

### Monday 7 Feb

The clouds have parted! Took their time, I must say . . .

Woke up feeling gloomy.

Gerald, who has agreed to be my unpaid, part-time secretary while he's at home, handed me the following letter this morning. Told me it had arrived in the first post. Quite excited as I began to read. This is what it said:

Dear Mr Plass,

Greetings in the name of he who empowers.

This is to inform you that prayerful consideration on the part of the church committee has revealed you to be God's chosen guest speaker on the occasion of our Autumn Church Family Weekend this year. Your message will be given on Friday the Eighth of September at 7:33 p.m. and should be *no more* than twenty-seven minutes in length, to include a final five-minute period in which signs following (excluding slaying in the Spirit and lengthy individual ministry please) may be manifested to and among the assembly. Your talk must be supported by appropriate Scriptural references (extracted from the Never Inflamatory Version of the Bible please) and needs to be broken into three easily comprehended sections, each beginning with the same letter.

Limited humour (mild only please) is allowable in the initial stages in order to demonstrate that Christians enjoy fun, but should be swiftly succeeded by admonitory and exhortational modes of address culminating in a controlled but movingly passionate appeal for changed lives at around the twenty minute mark. Please stress that such changes should occur within a denominational context. Some past speakers have, regrettably, held the wire fence down, as it were, thereby allowing errant members of our assembly to migrate to spiritual pastures new. We would ask you, in this connection, to emphasize the God-given authority of our church elders, and the fact that your task is simply to point the attending church members in their direction.

Please *do not* invite questions as these invariably disrupt time schedules, and tend to have an unsettling effect on those who are not yet truly wedded to our understanding and exposition of the Word.

We wish you to speak on the subject: 'ALLOWING THE SPIRIT TO WORK'. Please feel free (within the above parameters) to follow the Lord's leading in the presentation of his word as it is ministered to you.

Please send details of the fee you are likely to demand in return for doing the Lord's work on this occasion, bearing in mind that in addition to being already heavily in debt as we await confirmation that certain faith enterprises are truly of God, we are likely to be out of pocket at the end of the event, and that all spare money is, in any case, generally sent to alleviate the suffering of sick and starving children whom no one cares about, perishing alone on dung-heaps in poverty-stricken parts of the world.

We will, of course, cover your travelling expenses. We plan to purchase and post to you a return ticket issued by the national coach company, the timetable of which indicates an ideal service leaving your home town at 5:30 a.m. on the Friday in question and making a scheduled stop at a town two miles distant from the conference centre at 6:30 p.m. in the evening. The last stage of your journey could be in the form of a brisk walk (not unacceptable after a day of motorized travel, I dare swear), or, if you should so decide, I believe there are taxis available from the town centre. It may well be, however, that you are reluctant to expend such a large proportion of your fee in this way.

You can, of course, in case of extreme difficulty, and only *if absolutely necessary,* contact us at the conference centre by phone, but I should point out that there is only one telephone, situated in the farthest recesses of an extensive and comprehensively locked cellar system beneath a completely different wing of the building from the one that we shall be using, and that the Centre manager, who is elderly, arthritic and less than amenable to special requests, allows no telephonic access to visitors. I feel sure you understand our reluctance to use up goodwill in this area. If you do decide to walk (and the decision is entirely yours), you should be with us by 7:00 p.m. at the latest, which would allow you a good half hour to explore the Centre, rest for a minute or two, eat your supper, which June Salmons will pour into a bowl to save and warm up for you, meet a few of the folks you will be speaking to, supervise a Getting To Know You Game, say a brief word to the children's group which begins its meeting just before ours and join the elders for a time of instruction and prayer before beginning your talk.

I estimate that there will be approximately three hundred folks present at the meeting. The hall we are using was originally one arm of an old cloister, and, although very long, is also very thin. As you can imagine, communicating with lines of four people stretching back for seventy-five rows is a stimulating challenge for a speaker, especially when no public address system is available, as is the case here. Please do speak up, as most of our elderly friends like to sit at the back for ease of egress if they become bored or in need of the facilities.

After the meeting please feel free to stay and chat with folks for as long as you wish, although we quite understand that you will need to return to town in good time to catch the coach which departs for your return journey at 9:30 p.m. that same evening. If you have heavy cases to lug back to town, just mention it to the elders, any one of whom will be pleased to offer very competitive rates.

Perhaps I should say, in passing, that accommodation is actually available at the Conference Centre, and, just in case that is a decision you wish to make, I am pleased to enclose the relevant price-list for your consideration. I am afraid that you would *not* benefit from the group-booking rate that members of our church will enjoy, and I also need to make it clear that if you do stay on as a paying guest your return coach ticket will no longer be valid, and you will therefore have to make alternative, and possibly very costly travel arrangements for yourself on the following day. The last thing we want is for you to end up out-of-pocket and feeling used. That wouldn't be very Christian, would it?

Please write back as soon as possible confirming your availability for this event and your agreement in the matters detailed in this letter.

Yours,
Dennis Floom
(For The Open Heart Fellowship)

P.S. Please enclose stamped addressed envelope with your reply for despatch of coach tickets.

Gerald must think I'm terribly naïve. Realized it wasn't a genuine letter as soon as I looked closely at the words on the paper and recognized the print from Gerald's machine. Was about to suggest that jokes about invitations to speak weren't really very funny at the moment, when he handed me another letter that had been sent through my publishers.

Couldn't believe it!

The letter came from a place called Bongalinga Creek in Western Australia, and it was to inform me that the joint churches of Bongalinga Creek were planning to stage a production of *The Theatrical Tapes of Leonard Thynn,* a book I wrote some years ago about putting on a play for our local drama festival. They apologized for the short notice, and said that because of a very recent, anonymous gift, offered specially for the purpose, they are able to invite me and Leonard to GO TO AUSTRALIA and be at a performance on the twenty-fourth of March this year, and THEY WILL PAY FOR EVERYTHING. Suggested that if I was happy to speak at a few meetings while I was there, they could probably PAY FOR ANNE TO COME AS WELL.

Could hardly speak for excitement. Had to run all the way up to the top of the house and all the way down again for no reason before all the popping, pinging springs in me settled down. Gerald says he'll come too and pay for himself if it all works out. Couldn't wait to tell Anne when she came in at lunchtime. Dreaded her pointing out some tedious wedding or funeral or something that would prevent us going. Needn't have worried. She said the only thing that would have got in the way of me going was if she hadn't been able to go. All three of us did a little dance round the kitchen. So exciting!

I'M AN INTERNATIONAL SPEAKER AND I'M GOING TO AUSTRALIA!

I'M GOING TO AUSTRALIA AND I'M AN INTERNATIONAL SPEAKER!

TO AUSTRALIA I'M GOING IN THE ROLE OF INTERNATIONAL SPEAKER!

SPEAKING IN AUSTRALIA IS WHAT I'M DOING ON AN INTERNATIONAL BASIS!

INTERNATIONAL SPEAKING IS THE BASIS ON WHICH I'M GOING TO AUSTRALIA!

Called Leonard this evening. Told him we were going to Australia and that he would be guest of honour at the play in Bongalinga Creek.

He said, 'Great! Will it involve being away the night?'

## Tuesday 8 Feb

In high spirits all day today.

Phone call this evening from the Reverend Spool, rector of St Dermot's at the other end of town.

He said, 'Ah, Mr Plass, may I say –'

'Call me Adrian.'

We international speakers are like that.

'Well, that is most kind, and you must feel free to address me as Vladimir.'

'Vladimir?'

'Vladimir, yes, that's right. Now, Adrian, I am ringing to ask if you might very kindly consider the possibility of favouring us with a visit here at St Dermot's on Sunday March the thirteenth. I do realize, of course, that a person as well known as yourself will already have a very full diary, but I just wondered . . .'

Replied as though flicking through a diary full of international trips. 'Well, let's have a look here. Yes, the Australian trip comes later in the month, so that's no problem . . .'

'Australia – my goodness, what a following you must have, Adrian. I suppose you travel all over the world, do you?'

'Well . . .' Laughed lightly as though I didn't want to make too much of it. 'I wouldn't say that.'

'You wouldn't say that! But I am quite sure it must be true!'

'Oh, no . . .'

'So you feel you may be able to squeeze us in on the thirteenth. It would cause much excitement in the church if it were possible.'

'Yes, I think I can help you there, er, Vladimir. I'll put it into the diary straightaway. That would be the morning service, presumably, would it?'

'Precisely!' said Reverend Spool, who seemed to find everything I said amazingly clever. 'The morning service, that's absolutely right – gosh yes! I really am most grateful, and you must let us know your normal fee for such an occasion. I firmly insist on that.'

'Oh, that's not a problem at all. By the way, Vladimir, I just wondered – your Christian name seems er . . .'

'Ah, well, yes, no, you see, yes, you're absolutely right, it is indeed an uncommon first name for an English Anglican clergyman, but the simple truth is that as a young, impressionable girl my poor dear mother eloped with a vodka salesman and I, believe it or not, was the product.'

'Oh.'

'Well, thank you once again.'

'Think nothing of it. So I'll see you on March thirteenth at, what – ten o'clock?'

'Ten o'clock is spot on! See you then, and thank you again so much for agreeing to do our children's talk. Goodbye.'

Had actually put the phone down before Spool's final words registered.

A children's talk?

Oh, well, if I can travel across the world to speak I shouldn't have any trouble with a few kids, should I?

## Wednesday 9 Feb

*before supper*

Spent a lot of time at work today thinking about my ministry generally and our trip abroad in particular. Be nice to reach out to people with the gift of healing. Must be wonderful to have a real healing ministry. Not that I'm complaining about what I do, of course. It's just that – well, it must be wonderful.

Got completely distracted by one of my favourite, very satisfying fantasies. It's a wonderful daydream.

*Dressed in a very smart suit, I'm walking slowly up the centre aisle of a huge, packed auditorium, while a band plays softly on the stage behind me. Yearning, pleading eyes try to catch mine as I pass. Imploring arms stretch out in the desperate hope that perhaps just the touch of my coat against the sufferer's fingers might bring healing. Eventually, I am confronted by a mere child in a wheelchair. She forces a smile onto her broken, pretty little face as she senses the aura of spiritual power that surrounds me. My eyes fill with compassionate tears as I lay a hand on the thin, twisted shoulder of this tiny victim of the Fall. 'What do you want of me?' I ask, in a deep, cosmically resonant sort of voice* (rather like the one in the lager adverts). *'I want to be able to walk,' she whispers. 'And so you shall,' I reply. 'And so you shall. In the name of Jesus – be healed!' Slowly, dramatically, she pushes herself to her feet, her pain-filled eyes alight with a new, radiant hope, and then, suddenly, she is running, running, running, along the length of the aisle and up onto the stage. Gasps of amazement are followed by loud and prolonged applause as I follow her into the spotlight, only to turn modestly away towards the darkness of the wings, my expression one of mingled exhaustion, joy and pain. For none can guess the draining personal cost of this great and selfless work. Who can tell –*

'Got 'ny tissues?'

Hate real life sometimes. Fancy having to move from a massive auditorium full of adoring, tragically needy people and a chronically sick child in a wheelchair – to Everett Glander with a cold. Especially as I only had one tissue left and I was about to use it to dry my eyes after being so moved by the thought of my great healing ministry. Really resented giving away my last paper handkerchief to someone who persistently refuses to be converted. Glander's been along to a few church things since he met Frank Braddock at our party a few years ago, but nothing seems to quite do the trick. If I didn't know God was perfect I'd say that he'd missed a few excellent opportunities with Glander. Wonder if he'd be any different if he was redeemed. Hope so. At the moment he has the knack of saying the one thing you really don't want to hear. That's what he did today after I'd given him my last tissue.

'Why don't you ask God to make my cold better – or do I not qualify for some reason? Or is it just that *he* hasn't found a cure for the common cold either? Or is it –'

'Everett, if God wanted to heal your cold, he could do it just like that.'

Snapped my fingers, then turned back to my work with what was supposed to be a that's-the-end-of-the-conversation sort of movement. Dreaded him continuing the conversation.

'Well, why would God *not* want to heal my cold, then, old chap?'

Looked at him. Because, I thought silently, he probably finds you as awkward and obnoxious as I do, and a miracle might finally provoke you into coming to church every Sunday, and then I'd have to put up with you for six days a week instead of only five. Unless, of course, we manage to set up a little denomination specially for people like you, called the Seventh Day Everett Glanderites, where members of the congregation raise their objections during worship instead of their arms.

'Because,' I said out loud, 'his will is sovereign, and he is all-knowing. It's probably better for you to have a cold than to not have one, in ways that are difficult for us to understand.'

Glander said, 'Why has your voice gone all high-pitched, Adrian? Something wrong with your throat?'

Muttered under my breath, 'There'll be something wrong with yours if I get my hands round it.'

'So what you're talking about,' rasped on Glander, 'is the old "Living in the Mystery" syndrome, right?'

'Well, I wouldn't put it quite like that, but –'

'All right, then, old man, you give me an example of a reason why it would be better for me to go on having a cold than be healed. Just one'll do.'

He leaned back, sucking his pencil, grinning infuriatingly. Racked my brains for something convincing. Tried to look as if I was calmly selecting one of many possible answers available to me.

I said, 'Well, er, for instance, you might be walking along the road on your way home tonight –'

'Always get the bus just outside the building, old boy.'

'All right, you might get on the bus tonight and happen to be sitting next to an international expert in medical research who –'

'Unlikely to get too many of them on the top deck of the Number 39 to Grey Prospect Road, in my humble view, old man.'

Gritted my teeth. 'Well, this one's a poor but very clever one who's on the brink of discovering – you know – what you said before, a cure for the common cold, and he looks at you sniffing away next to him, and all of a sudden feels inspired. Suddenly the last bit of the jigsaw falls into place, and when he gets home he writes it all down, and before long millions of people have their colds cured, all because God didn't heal you at the moment when you thought it was a good idea.'

Felt quite pleased with myself.

'Yeah, but if he wanted to,' persisted Glander, reminding me of one of those road-drills that carry on their insane clattering right over the last bit of a television programme you particularly wanted to hear, 'he could heal all those millions of people anyway. Or have I got it all wrong?'

'No – I mean, yes, he could.'

'So why doesn't he?'

'Well, because er ... He doesn't heal them because ...'

Screamed silently at God:

WELL, WHY DON'T YOU HEAL THEM, FOR GOODNESS SAKE? IF GLANDER CAN WORK IT OUT, WHY CAN'T YOU?

Glander said, 'Tell you what – just in case it turns out there isn't an international expert on medical research who needs me to sit next to him on the bus tonight, how about praying for my cold to go away now?'

'Now?'

'Now.'

Somehow managed to mumble a miserable prayer, but I hadn't the slightest faith in it being answered. Besides which, if I'm honest, I really hadn't even a remote interest in seeing the state of Everett's nasal passages improved. Part of me rather hoped he might develop complications and die. I can't seem to make Christianity work at all when I'm with him. He sniffed loudly and obviously for the rest of the morning, then he went out to the chemist's at lunchtime and came back with a box of tissues. Paid my one tissue back to me very obviously.

Thank you, God – I don't think!

He could have backed me up, couldn't he? Rather hoping that it'll end like one of those Christian paperbacks, with Everett phoning me later to say that he's healed, and we'll both break down and sob together ...

## later

*8 p.m. (after supper)*

Anne shouted through just now to say Everett was on the phone. Rushed out to the hall very excited.

'Just called to tell you,' said Everett, 'that a mighty miracle hath occurred.'

'You mean your cold is ... ?'

'That's right. My cold's no better at all. So, presumably it won't be long before the papers are full of this wonderful new cure you were talking about.'

'Everett, you *know* that was only an ex –'

'I must say, though, Adrian, they're producing a very strange breed of international expert in medical research these days. The one sitting next to me on the bus tonight was the spitting image of a very fat lady with a Charlie Chaplin moustache who happens to live just down the road from me, and I have to be honest and say that, for someone who was just about to crack the medical problem of the century, she didn't seem very excited about my cold, old man. Quite the opposite, in fact. Still, there we are. See you tomorrow – if I'm well enough, that is.'

Went to bed feeling very depressed.

## Thursday 10 Feb

Told Anne and Gerald about Glander over breakfast this morning. I said, 'Why couldn't God have just healed his stupid cold and shut him up? I've got to face his big ugly mouth all day today.'

Anne said, 'It does seem a shame you're wasting so much compassion on him, darling, You'd think that all the warmth and love and genuine concern and goodwill that you pour out in his direction would have left him with no choice but to be healed. In future I shouldn't bother to waste all that positive energy on people you see every day. I should save it for people at your meetings. Don't you agree, Gerald?'

Couldn't help thinking Anne was rather overstating the case.

Gerald handed me an envelope with something written on the back. He said, 'How right you are, Mum, and I've written a little poem for Mr E. Bass, much loved lay reader and author of The Scared Dairy, to read out at his very next meeting.'

Read the poem out loud.

> 'Assist me in this new resolve, oh, Lord,
> That those who know and love and suffer me,
> Shall one day, through a miracle of Grace,
> Enjoy the warmth I use in ministry.'

Yes, all right, all right . . .

Went to work knowing that, however wrong my attitude might have been, if I had to put up with another day of Glander's sarcasm I'd really give him something to be healed of. Luckily he was off sick today, so that was all right.

Praise God!

Still couldn't stop thinking about healing all day, though. When I got home I asked Gerald to tell me seriously what he thought about the whole thing.

'Dad,' he said, 'I have thought about that a bit, and it seems to me that, when it comes to things like healing, people tend to rewrite the Bible to fit the way they want things to be. Especially the things Jesus said and did. It beats me how some folk can line up the things they do with what they read in the gospels. There's a sort of religious stubbornness that won't let the straightforwardness of Jesus' approach be a factor in the equation of real day-to-day living. I think it's probably a fear of facing the cosmic shock you get when you open your eyes and actually confront the fact that God really did become a man.'

Totally gobsmacked by this speech. Amazing! Can this really be the same Gerald who, not so very long ago, crept up behind me in the hall, put a raw egg in the hood of my anorak just as I was about to go out in the rain and then laughed himself sick when I came back and said that some huge bird must have laid it from a great height onto the top of my head just as I was pulling the hood up? Hope he doesn't get *too* serious.

Later, Gerald handed me another of these pieces of work he's been doing on the word processor. He said, 'Take a look at this chunk from Not-Luke, Dad. This is the sort of thing I meant about people rewriting Scripture. This must be the way it happened if some Christians I know have got it right.'

This is what Gerald had written:

A man with leprosy cometh and kneeleth before him and saith, 'Lord, if thou art willing thou canst make me clean.' Jesus reacheth out his hand and toucheth the man. 'I am willing,' he saith. 'Be clean!'

And behold, Jesus strolleth away rejoicing, but the leper haileth him with an loud voice, saying, 'Er, excuse me, mayhap it hath escaped thy notice, but I am still an leper. An small point, I know, but important to me.'

And Jesus hisseth through his teeth with vexation and replieth, 'Knoweth thou not that I am heavily into holistic healing? Good heavens, thou must indeed be well naïve if thou thinkest that healing concerneth thy body only. Keepest thou not up with current literature on the subject?'

The man saith, 'All I knoweth is that I was an leper five minutes ago, and behold, I am still an leper.'

'Well,' asserteth Jesus, 'despite thine complaints, thou art, in a very real sense, no longer an leper.'

'Oh, terrific!' persisteth the man, waxing sore sarcastic. 'But I *am* still an leper in the trivial but equally real sense that bits of me have droppeth off, and thou seemest incapable of replacing them.'

Then Jesus snorteth and demandeth, 'Why doth there always have to be one? All right, mate, there existeth a number of possibilities, none of which, I mighteth add, constituteth a failure on the part of myself or any other member of the management team. Counteth them off on thy fingers.'

'It'll have to come to less than three, then,' saith the leper.

Jesus ignoreth him.

'One, thou lackest faith – highly likely. Two, thou hast failed to claim thy healing, a common one, that. Three, thou hast been specially chosen to benefit others through thine own suffering – congratulations. Four, thine healing is to be in the form of death. Byeee! Five, thou art called but not chosen – tough! Anyway, I must departeth. I am up for a big catering contract and the size of the budget challengeth me greatly.'

He goeth, and the leper gathereth himself together, and repeateth over and over to himself, 'I am not an leper! I am not an leper! I am not an leper ...' And behold, from that day forth, he becameth known throughout that country as the Mad Leper.

Don't think I have to worry too much about Gerald getting over-serious!

Anne said tonight, 'I don't know why you're getting such a bee in your bonnet about bodies being healed. That doesn't seem to be your job at the moment. It's true the Reginald and thingy meeting was a disaster, but you know from other meetings you've done, and your books, that God has chosen you to help him heal people's feelings and tensions and worries through making them laugh, and cry a bit and relax. A lot of folk would give their eye-teeth to be able to do that.'

Said to God tonight, 'I expect Anne's right as usual. I should be grateful, I know. It's just that – well, you can't actually see healed feelings jump out of wheelchairs. I'm not complaining ...'

'Yes, you are,' said God.

## Friday 11 Feb

Very uneasy about this children's talk I've so foolishly agreed to do. Something tells me I should have rung Spool straight back and made it clear that only a platoon of crazed mercenaries armed with sub-machine-guns would be able to threaten me into addressing one of those ego-bludgeoning groups of small children that you see every now and then chewing up speakers who know nothing about what they're doing. Asked Anne if she thought I'd be all right. She said, 'No, but you promised. Why did you say you'd do it?' I'm going to ring Vladimir and tell him straight out I can't do it. Probably ring him tomorrow.

## Saturday 12 Feb

Had an amazing phone call this morning from a lady called Angela in Manchester who'd got my number through directory enquiries. At first I was a bit puzzled and nervous about the way the conversation was going. She told me that her father, Ron, went into hospital last year with a serious illness, and was told that he only had two or three months to live. Ron was deeply depressed, not just about his illness, but about his faith.

Angela said, 'He kept asking all these questions over and over again, and nothing I said made much difference. I mean, I couldn't think what to say for the best. It was awful. I got so upset. Both of us did – Mum and me.'

'What sort of questions?'

'Oh, all kinds. Was he really saved? Did God really care about him? Was he praying properly? Had he done all the things you have to do to make sure you get into heaven? I know it sounds a bit silly, but Dad got himself into a right old stew about what was going to happen after he – well, after he went, you know. He started reading the Bible sort of – I don't know how to put it – *feverishly,* as though he was fuelling up for some long journey, but I'm pretty sure he hardly understood a word of what he was reading. It was just panic, if you know what I mean.'

Wondered what this was all leading up to.

I said, 'And what happened next?'

'Well, that's why I'm phoning. I gave him your book to read – your diary book. Mum bought it for me for my birthday, so I had it on the shelf at home.'

Cleared my throat uneasily. 'So, you er . . . gave your father my book to read in the hospital.'

'That's right, yes.'

'And he – '

'He laughed himself to death, Adrian. My Dad laughed himself to death.'

Felt a bit worried. Wanted to ask if this was a good thing or a bad thing, but didn't like to. I could hear Angela was nearly crying on the other end of the phone. I said, 'So, he did – he did enjoy it, then?'

'Oh, Adrian, he really relaxed after that. I think it helped him realize most of those big problems of his were made by men – or people, I mean. You're not supposed to say that sort of thing any more, are you? – not by God. Poor old Dad had somehow forgotten that God loves him, I think, and reading your book gave him back his spiritual common sense, if it's all right to call it that. And, you know, he kept that little book on his bedside locker right up to the very end. Even when he got too bad to read for himself, he used to get me to read bits out to him, and you could hear this little wheezy laugh right in the middle of him. I reckon when he walked into heaven God must have smiled at Dad and said, 'What are you laughing about, Ron?' And Dad will've answered, 'Sorry, it's just this book I was reading . . .' Anyway, I rang just to thank you really, that's all.'

I mumbled, 'No – thank *you* for ringing. Thank you.'

Meant it.

Told Anne about the call. Tears came to her eyes. She said, 'And you moan about not having a healing ministry. God spoils you – you know that, don't you?'

## Sunday 13 Feb

This morning Edwin asked the congregation to get into small groups and talk about what we'd want to rescue most if our houses caught fire.

Anne said to me, 'Which of your most valued things would you go back for?'

I said, 'You.'

Multitudinous Brownie points, *and* I meant it!

## Monday 14 Feb

Both remembered Valentine's day! A miracle!

Nervous about the first meeting of my support group this evening.

Went quite well in the end. Edwin said we should start off with a small group and build up gradually, so tonight there was just Anne, Gerald, Edwin, Richard and Doreen Cook, Leonard Thynn – I was a bit surprised that Edwin chose Leonard, fond though I am of him – and me.

(Edwin said that if Victoria and Stenneth Flushpool hadn't been away on their African mission trip they would certainly have been part of the group. Amazing to think how much Victoria has changed since we first knew her. There was a time when she made the Pharisees look like angels of mercy. Nowadays, Stenneth is no longer forced to hide his copies of *Balsa Modelling Monthly* under the nuptial mattress because of his wife's belief that he is unhealthily ensnared by full-frontal photographs of Sopwith Camels made of wood. Miss them both really.)

Quite apprehensive, and suddenly very embarrassed at the idea of being the centre of attention in such an obvious way.

Everyone except Leonard arrived on time at about seven-thirty. Needn't have worried about being the centre of attention. They all got chatting immediately, as though it was just a social occasion and they'd forgotten why we were meeting.

Doreen, for instance, who was in a very stiff mood anyway, for some reason, was getting very worked up about unsuitable videos being available to young people in the High Street shops – one of her hobby-horses. Funny thing, although I agree completely with just about everything Doreen says on this subject, the more she talks about it, the more part of me wants to rush out, hire an unsuitable video and make it available to a young person. I think there must be something wrong with my attitude . . .

Gerald listened for a while, then said, 'Actually, Doreen, there's a film showing at the Curzon in town that I think you'd disapprove of, and it's got a "U" certificate, so children of any age can go to it. In fact I actually *saw* small children going in on my way home tonight.'

Anne and I know that slight change in Gerald's voice all too well. We braced ourselves. Doreen leaned forward, the light of holy battle in her eyes.

She said, 'What sort of film is it, Gerald?'

Gerald shook his head worriedly and said, 'I hardly dare tell you, Doreen. It's – well, it's so awful ...'

'Gerald, remember that you are covered.'

I read in my son's eyes his decision to sacrifice the opportunity to make comments about third party fire and theft for the sake of whatever else he had in mind. Nodding solemnly, he continued slowly and gravely.

'Well, all right. It's a story about a family violently ripped apart by cruelty and death. It's a tale of guns and fire and the blind fear that fuels panic-stricken flight. It's a tale of homelessness and isolation and the death of innocence.'

Dramatic silence. Doreen took a notebook and pen from her handbag, and set her mouth in a thin grim line (Like Biggles when bandits appear at two o'clock, Gerald commented later).

'What is the name of the film?' she demanded, with a sort of verbal roll of drums.

'*Bambi,*' said Gerald.

Doreen's reactions to Gerald's nonsense never cease to amaze me. She simply closed her notebook, clicked her Biro, and replaced both items in her handbag. She then sat back in her chair quite unmoved, as though the forty second capsule of time containing this little interchange had never actually existed.

I've noticed this before with people who are in permanently religious mode. It's as if their personality computers have been programmed in a very limited way. In this case, Doreen, having pressed her SEARCH button and keyed in GERALD HAS MADE A JOKE, had received a message on her mental screen which read: INVALID REQUEST: NO SUCH FILE: GERALD-HAS-MADE-A-JOKE NOT KNOWN: TRY COATES, and abandoned the whole thing.

Richard, on the other hand, nodded as if he understood perfectly, and said, 'Ah yes, I believe that is the word commonly employed to describe young ladies who are, shall we say – wanton.'

All stared at Richard.

'I refer,' he explained, colouring a little, 'to those scenes that one cannot avoid witnessing inadvertently on the television from time to time, where a man is said to be out walking with "some new bambi on his arm".'

Anne said gently, 'I think the word you're thinking of is "bimbo", Richard. Bambi is a little deer ...'

'Expensive, you mean?'

'No-no, *Bambi* is the name of a little deer ...'

'But in that case, why on earth – '

Just as Richard's confusion began to acquire a truly surrealistic quality, the doorbell interrupted proceedings, thank goodness. Answered the door. On the step was a figure leaning unsteadily on a stick, its head, arms and legs covered in bandages. A frail, quavery voice emerged from a crack in the bandages around the face.

'Please pray for me to be healed.'

I just don't believe Thynn sometimes. Told him to come in and stop being stupid. Incredible! Sat himself down in the sitting-room, bandages and all, and explained that he'd thought it would give my talks a 'bit of a boost' if he came along to the odd meeting in his 'cripple outfit' and got miraculously healed on the spot.

He said, 'It'd put God in a better light, wouldn't it?'

'But, Leonard,' I almost screamed, 'that would be telling lies, wouldn't it? We don't want people to believe in God because of a lie, do we?'

'Oh, don't we?' said Leonard, sounding genuinely surprised.

'You mean it's all right to tell the truth about everything?'

'Of course it is.'

'Everything?'

'Yes.'

'Oh, I see. Good! In that case I can tell everyone why I thought it was all right to tell lies. You see – well, you know the other night when Anne was away and we watched the late film at your house, Adrian?'

Glanced round nervously at the others and said warily, 'Ye-e-es.'

'Well, you know you and Gerald drank a whole bottle of wine each and I didn't have any because I can't?'

Glanced even more nervously at Anne. 'A bit of an exaggeration, I think, Leonard, don't you?'

Gerald said, 'Mmm, that is a bit of an exaggeration, Leonard. Dad had one and a half bottles – I only had about three glasses.'

'Oh, that's right, sorry, Gerald,' said Leonard, 'you were drinking out of a glass, I'd forgotten that. Adrian was lying on the sofa swigging straight out of the bottle – I mean bottles plural.'

Felt my face flaming. So much for wanting Thynn to tell the truth! How were my support group going to deal with this mental picture of the great evangelist sprawled across the living-room at midnight with a bottle of booze attached to his mouth like a baby's dummy?

'Just a minute, I don't understand,' said Anne, 'you can't possibly have drunk both bottles. There were only two to start with, and I remember seeing one left when I got the Hoover out the next afternoon.'

'Oh, I forgot that,' said Leonard, 'but I remember now. Adrian said he'd have to nip out quick in the morning and get another one to put in the cupboard so you wouldn't know.'

Mentally checked my life-insurance policies. Surely Thynn could see that not telling lies doesn't necessarily mean you have to tell the *whole truth*.

'Anyway, just before you finished the second bottle, you started talking about your meetings, and you got up and stood on the sofa with a Bible balanced on your head and said you were going to bring people to faith by hook or by crook. And when I asked you what that meant, you said it meant that it doesn't matter whether people are converted by bishops or con men. Then, just as you were going to say something else you fell off the sofa and rolled onto the floor and lay there singing "Roll me over, lay me down and do it again", and you said it was an old chorus about being slain in the Spirit. And that's why I thought it didn't matter if we told lies. Sorry.'

Felt strangely calm.

I said, 'Well, there we are then. It's nice to have this little group of people here to witness three significant endings – the end of my ministry, the end of my marriage and the end of Leonard Thynn's life when the rest of you have gone.' Shook my head in despair. 'I'm ever so sorry, everybody. Sorry, Anne. I can't tell you how embarrassed I am by all that stuff about the other night, especially going out and getting another bottle and all that. I really suggest the best thing is that you all go quietly home and we just forget about the whole thing. Sorry ...'

'We can still have the food, though, can't we?' said Thynn sensitively.

Edwin cleared his throat and leaned forward, clasping his hands and resting his arms on his knees. He studied the floor as he began to speak.

'Now look, Adrian, the reason I chose the people who are here in this room to be the nucleus of your support group is that they are all people who love you. And we don't love you because you're perfect. You're not – any more than I am. We're fond of you because of lots of things, and despite a few other things. Do you understand that?' He looked up at me. I nodded, feeling a bit weepy. 'We don't want to support a writer or a speaker. We want to support *you*, the real you, not some shined up, falsely virtuous character who doesn't really exist. The things that happened the other night when Anne was away – well, let's just say I would have been embarrassed as well if they'd been described in front of other people, but, let's face it, every one of us here has almost certainly got some personal skeleton in the cupboard that we wouldn't be at all keen to put on public view. Something that God has forgiven but still makes us feel a bit guilty sometimes. Isn't that right, everybody?'

He looked enquiringly around at the other members of the group. Anne, Gerald and Leonard nodded agreement straight-away.

Richard looked terrified. Clutched his Bible to his chest with both arms like a comforter and said, 'Er, well, of course, Scripture does allow that a – a thorn in the flesh may be allowed by the Lord for purposes of growth in the area of humility, but er ...'

'It's all right, Richard,' said Edwin, smiling a little, 'you don't have to tell us what your particular thorn actually is. I'm just making the point that we've all got at least a thorn or two – *and* a load of marks from old thorns that God has got rid of, so none of us can afford to judge anyone else, can we?'

'Oh, no,' replied Richard, relieved to be back on safe ground, 'there is certainly no question of judgment of others. I – I would like to express my full support to Adrian in his ministry and I – I agree with all that Edwin er – all that Edwin has said about er ... it.'

I think Doreen might have liked to inform us that those who are in Christ are a new creation, and therefore without sin, but she contented herself with nodding in a slow, overtly compromising sort of way. 'We shall support Adrian as he seeks to do the Lord's work in every way possible,' she said.

Gerald whispered in my ear, 'I'm glad we're not going to compare thorns behind the bike-sheds.'

'The point is, Adrian,' continued Edwin, 'that as you get even more well known, I'm afraid most people will tend to lose sight of the real person behind the books and talks – they always do – and that's not going to be easy for you. That's what this group is for. We'll all still be dealing with the Adrian Plass that's frail and human and exactly the same as us – the person that we love. I think it's good that Leonard told us about what happened the other night. It means we start clean – and, with a bit of luck, we'll stay clean.'

Doreen said, 'I am sure, Edwin, that when you speak of a "bit of luck", you are actually referring to the Grace of God?'

'Well, yes,' sighed Edwin, 'of course, Doreen, I meant that we shall stay clean by the Grace of God.'

'With a bit of luck,' added Gerald, making most of us laugh.

After that the meeting went well. We decided that the group would meet as and when needed, but at least once in every three months or so. Each session was to consist of a report from me on things that had already happened, including problems and difficulties that needed prayer and advice, followed by a look at my forthcoming diary and discussion about the future. We agreed that any of us could contribute any view we wanted as long as we were ready to discover that we were wrong.

Hmmm . . .

Finally, someone – a different person each time – would do a short Bible-study before we prayed together. Edwin said that he would 'enrich' the group by adding one or two other people as time went by, but refused to say who they might be. Didn't quite like to ask if Norma would be one of them. Not that she's – you know, special to me in any way . . .

Prayed for a while about a talk I'm doing in Derby on February sixteenth, and an outreach dinner on Saturday the nineteenth. Been trying to pretend to myself that the children's talk doesn't exist, but thought I'd better mention it. Hoped someone would have a word from God to say I shouldn't do it, but no one did. Think I'll cancel it anyway. I'll definitely call Vladimir tomorrow.

Had coffee and relaxed and chatted after that. One or two highlights. When Richard asked Anne to pass him the concordance, Thynn said, 'Oh, great, we're going to have a sing-song, are we?'

Incredibly, he wasn't joking.

When Anne explained what a concordance was, Leonard was absolutely scandalized. Said to Edwin, 'All those weeks you've stood up the front going from passage to passage to passage about the same thing, and I've always thought, "Blimey! I wish I knew my Bible well enough to do that." And all the time you were using a – a camcorder.'

'Concordance,' corrected Edwin, 'and you're dead right, Leonard, I cheat every time.'

A little embarrassing when Gerald took it upon himself to tell everyone that he thought I ought to be fully aware of the rules that govern something he calls the 'White Envelope Game'.

He said, 'I've seen Dad playing it ever so many times without realizing what it is, but I should think most Christian speakers play it at one time or another. What happens is this. The meeting finishes, and the bloke who's done the talk – let's call him Cedric the Speaker – knows that, at some point soon, one of the organizers is almost certain to approach him holding a white envelope with his name written on the front. And, of course, Cedric's very keen on this because the envelope has usually got some cash or a cheque in it. The trouble is – the first and strictest rule of the White Envelope Game is that the speaker isn't allowed to give any indication that he's even remotely interested in receiving such a thing, so he begins – '

Anne interrupted. 'If the time comes to leave and the envelope hasn't appeared yet, Cedric begins a sort of have-I-said-goodbye-to-everyone? dance, which consists of going around shaking hands in an impressively conscientious way, hoping that when he comes to the one who's got the cash, his or her memory will be jogged enough to get it out and part with it.'

Gerald looked admiringly at his mother. 'Good one, Mumsy! You're absolutely right. Anyway, sooner or later the person in question – let's call him George – approaches Cedric with the white envelope clutched in his hand, and it's at this point that the game begins in earnest.'

'Gerald,' I broke in, 'I'm quite sure that no one else wants to hear all this nonsense.'

Looked around seeking confirmation, but Edwin said, 'Oh, yes we do! Carry on, Gerald. As an occasional White Envelope distributor *and* collector myself, I find this all most interesting.'

'Right, well, having, as Mum said, hung around for ages to make sure he actually gets offered the White Envelope, Cedric now appears to be strangely incapable of perceiving the object when someone is virtually holding it under his nose. In fact, at this point Cedric will usually set off through the door, apparently leaving, but actually confident in the knowledge that he'll be stopped long before he gets outside.

'And, naturally, he is. Deeply impressed by the fact that Cedric the Speaker didn't miss even the humblest soul in his farewells, and that he's too ethereally absorbed to even *notice* money when it's offered to him, the holder of the White Envelope briskly pursues the saintly figure, stopping him in the porch and saying something along the following lines:

'"We thought – well, we just wanted to – you know – say thank you for – well, for coming and – well, we'd like you to accept this with our – you know ..."

'The time has now come for Cedric to role-play a subtle and quite endearing combination of confusion and puzzlement. He holds the envelope in his hand, peering curiously at it as though the concepts of "white" and "envelope" are completely new in his experience.

'"What on earth – ? What's this? Good heavens, I never expected ..."

'"Oh, it's just – just nothing," says George shyly, "really it's nothing – it's just nothing – just a little something to say – you know ..."

'A sudden revelation seems to hit Cedric like a thunderbolt. He's being given some money! Well, what a profound, totally unexpected, mind-numbing shock! He shakes his head with the wonder of it all.

'"You didn't have to give me this," he murmurs, nevertheless holding tightly on to the envelope as he speaks, "I certainly didn't do it for – well, for any sort of reward, except, of course, just knowing that the Lord is ..."

'"Oh, we know that!" replies George hurriedly, embarrassed that a spiritual giant of this magnitude should be burdened with something as vulgar as money, "but, for your ministry – well, just a small gift."

'Cedric quickly tucks the unopened envelope away in the inside pocket of his jacket as if its contents are of no interest to him whatsoever. It's quite possible, his manner suggests, that he will completely forget it's there and *never* bother to open it up to see what it contains. One more firm clasp of George's hand and a momentary engagement of his eyes in order to convey godly depth, prayerful good wishes, and warm gratitude, then outside and into the car for a dignified pulling away, a final wave and a sudden halt at a quiet spot three streets away to drag the White Envelope from the inside pocket and *rip it open* to find out how much he's got . . .'

Leonard said, 'Blimey! It's hard work being a speaker, innit? I don't think I could do all that.'

'Richard and I would be pleased to offer ministry to you, Adrian, if this pattern of deceit and wrong motivation is truly part of your experience,' offered Doreen.

Was about to reply but Edwin chuckled and said, 'Come on now, Doreen, that was a bit of a caricature that Gerald gave us, but I don't mind confessing that it wasn't so far from how I was a few years ago when the old shoe was pinching most of the time. You didn't want to look greedy, but you really hoped there'd be some cash involved because then you could do something unusual like – eat. Even now my motives are pretty mixed up. Always will be, I should think, but God knows about all that, because,' he finished simply, 'I tell him.'

Doreen cleared her throat slightly worriedly. 'Richard, have you er, encountered any of these er . . . feelings?'

Richard said, 'My own experience on those few occasions that I have performed a visiting speaker's role have differed from the hypothetical Cedric's in one particular way.'

Doreen looked relieved. 'And what is that difference?'

'Well,' replied Richard slowly, 'I never rip the envelope apart – I open it carefully so that I can save it and use it again . . .'

## Tuesday 15 Feb

Everett Glander is like one of those splinters in the hand that you should have taken out when it first went in, but you didn't and now it's got so far under your skin that you can't shift it. Wish he'd either move to China or get converted and go to some church that isn't ours.

Hate me hating him ...

## Wednesday 16 Feb

Back at my hotel in Derby after speaking this evening. What a day!

I have had some extremely annoying conversations in my time, but this morning's encounter with a man who is paid regular money to supply the public with information about trains just about takes the biscuit. I realize that more and more people are being trained as counsellors, but if there aren't enough jobs to go round at the moment I really don't see why they should be inflicted on the general public.

Granted, it was me who made the mistake in the first place – I accept that. I forgot to set the alarm and ended up flinging myself down the road with a heavy case to the station. Flung myself on to the platform and found what I thought was the Derby train just about to go. Flung myself and case on, discovered instantly that it was the non-stop Flaxton train, flung myself off, remembered my case was still on, flung myself round intending to fling myself back on, and found that the train was moving out. Wanted to die. Worn out with flinging myself around. Knew I'd have to get the next train to Flaxton to get my case back, and then take a cross-country train to Derby. Just time if I was lucky with connections. Naïvely thought that I could find out about the next train to Flaxton from the travel centre. Arrived at the desk in a bit of a state, to find a young man with what I can only describe as a soppy grin on his face nodding at me like a toy dog in the back of a car. As far as I recall the dialogue went as follows.

ME: (WILDLY) Which train do I get to Flaxton?

MAN: (SLOWLY AND INSIGHTFULLY) Okay – which train do you want to get to Flaxton?

ME: (INCREDULOUS PAUSE) One that goes there, please. Soon! What are you talking about? Do you think I want a Flaxton train that *doesn't* go to Flaxton? Are you stupid or something?

MAN: (STILL NODDING AND SMILING) Thank you for sharing your anger with me.

ME: (COMPLETELY LOSING MY RAG AND HOPING HE DOESN'T READ CHRISTIAN BOOKS) I'll be sharing a left hook with you in a minute, if you –

MAN: (INTERRUPTING) Can I ask you something?

ME: (FAINTLY) *You* want to ask *me* something?

MAN: Do I remind you of your father?

ME: (APPROACHING HYSTERIA) No, you don't remind me of my father. My father was sane and helpful. Look! It's very simple really. I've left my case on the Flaxton train and I've got to get it back in time to get to Derby because I'm speaking there tonight. All right?

MAN: Okay, let's just unpack this.

ME: (ARRIVING AT HYSTERIA) I'd love to unpack it, you dozy pillock, but it's on its way to Flaxton!

MAN: (THERAPEUTICALLY APPRECIATIVE) Mmmm, oka-a-a-y! Humour's always good.

ME: (HAMMERING ON THE DESK WITH MY FISTS) Never mind humour! Never mind anything else! Just tell me which train I get to Flaxton. Tell me now!

MAN: May I tell you what I'm hearing you say?

ME: (A LOW GROWLING NOISE) Rrrrr ...

MAN: What I feel I'm hearing you say – what I think I'm hearing the child in you say, friend, is that you don't want to go to Derby at all, and that's why you unconsciously made the

51

decision to leave your case on the Flaxton train. You actually never want to see that suitcase again. Am I resonating?

ME: (DEFEATED – HEAD DOWN ON THE COUNTER, MORE OR LESS SOBBING) Look, couldn't you please just tell me when the next train to Flaxton goes? That's all I want – I just want to go to Flaxton. Please lemme go to ...

MAN: (WITH WARM APPROVAL) All *ri-i-ight!* That's good, let it all out. Exteriorize the pain and we can deal with it together. (COMPASSIONATELY AND WITH IMMENSE SIGNIFICANCE) I guess that in a deeply real sense you've been wanting that case to become Flaxton's problem for a very, very long time. Am I right? (PAUSE – SUDDENLY EFFICIENT) Okay, well, I suggest you come back in a week's time, and in the meantime I'd like you to do some work on how you think you'd relate to Derby if it was a girl you were taking to the pictures. Who would pay? Would you sit in the back row? Might there be a subsequent pizza situation? That sort of thing. Now let me see ... (CONSULTS A DIARY) Yes, I can fit you in at eleven o'clock on Wednesday morning. And please – (PLAYFULLY) no spillage. Agreed?

ME: (HOMICIDALLY CALM) I really do suggest that, for your own sake, you should listen ever so carefully to what I am about to say. You are a person who is paid to provide information about trains to customers who need it. I, on the other hand, am a customer who needs a very small item of that information. If you do not provide a simple, factual answer to the next question that I ask, I promise you that I shall climb over to the side where you are, kneel on your chest, and make you eat the whole of the very substantial British Rail timetable that lies between us here on the counter. Now – when does the next train for Flaxton depart from this station?

PAUSE

MAN: Nine o'clock.

ME: Thank you for sharing that information with me.

Managed to get my case back and get to Derby all right in the end, but I was all hot and bothered by the time I got to the church where I was speaking. Stood out in the entrance porch for a little while signing books for people coming in.

Most embarrassing incident occurred.

A lady came up to me, held out one of my books, and said, 'Would you mind signing this for my friend, Eileen, only she's – well, she's inside.'

Pictured Eileen sitting in some lonely prison cell, and wrote in the book:

TO EILEEN
MAY YOU, BY SOME MIRACLE, BE FREE EVEN IN THAT PLACE.

Gave it back to the lady, who stared at what I'd written for a second, then said, 'No, no, I mean she's inside the church – she went in before me ...'

Got her a new book and changed the message to BEST WISHES. Felt a real fool.

Good evening after that. People really seemed to eat up the idea that God loved them.

Later in the week, when I told Edwin the 'inside' story, he said that he knew the church in question, and thought I'd probably got it right the first time.

Tried to repent of my crossness with the British Rail man, but I didn't find it easy. I know Jesus never sinned, but I'm pretty sure that bloke would have stretched him close to breaking point.

## Thursday 17 Feb

Couldn't stop thinking about this children's talk all the way back from Derby. Must phone Reverend Spool. All becoming a bit of a nightmare. Spoiling all my enjoyment of thinking about Australia. Too tired tonight – do it tomorrow ...

## Friday 18 Feb

Finally summoned up the courage to phone Vladimir Spool, but – PRAISE GOD! – he wasn't in.

Gerald, who was sitting by the fire with a book, looked up as I put the phone down and said, 'Is this vicar bloke really called Vladimir?'

'Yes.'

'Do you know if he was ever a smoker?'

Sensed that a very, very bad joke was imminent.

'No, why?'

'Because if he was, I bet I know what his congregation nick-named him.'

'And what might that have been?'

'Vlad the Inhaler.'

## Saturday 19 Feb

Off to speak at an outreach dinner this evening with Thynn, who said he wanted to have a go at selling books for me, and Gerald, who, apart from anything else, likes free dinners.

Always feel a bit uneasy about these outreach affairs. When I think of all the planning and work and prayer culminating in me standing up for half an hour and saying silly things, I get quite panicky. Felt even more nervous this time, because the lady organizing the dinner, somebody called Eve Worthington, had said on the phone that they were expecting the vast majority of the people who came to be non-Christians who had 'never been exposed to the raw Gospel' before. Not at all sure I was capable of producing the 'raw Gospel' for them to be exposed to. As we drove up the motorway, Gerald said I shouldn't get too worried because, in his experience, anticipated 'vast majorities' of non-Christians almost always resolve themselves into rather small minorities when it comes to the crunch.

He was absolutely right.

When we got to the hotel where the dinner was happening I asked Eve Worthington, who turned out to be a jolly little round ball of a person, how many of the diners were Christians by her reckoning. Tried to sound as if I desperately hoped they would *all* be non-Christians so that I could expose them to the r. G. and convert every one.

She whispered confidentially in my ear, 'Well, it hasn't worked out quite as we'd hoped, I'm afraid.'

Thought – Yesss!

Said, 'Oh, I'm *very* disappointed to hear that. It'll be nearly all Christians, then, will it?'

'Actually, there's only one non-Christian here,' said Eve.

Deeply thrilled, but a little surprised. The gap between a 'vast majority' and 'one' seemed a bit dramatic, to say the least.

'His name's Brian,' whispered Eve, 'and he's a neighbour of ours. I asked him to come right in the middle of my husband George getting covered in oil and grease fixing his car when it wouldn't start one Saturday, so he couldn't really refuse, could he? He'd be so useful in the Kingdom – he's a bank manager.'

Obviously felt it unnecessary to decode this cryptic statement. Brought her mouth even closer to my ear, and hissed enthusiastically, 'He's very close, you know! We've sat you opposite him at dinner.' Drew her head back, smiling and nodding significantly at me. My heart sank. I always turn into a worm in the presence of bank managers, and I never know what to say to people I'm supposed to 'do my stuff' on. Really dreaded dinner.

Went to find the toilet before sitting down (at the dinner-table, I mean). Just stood by the wash basins talking to God. 'I feel useless,' I said. 'I feel nervous and stupid and ugly and faithless and I want to go home.'

'Hallelujah! Go forth in victory!' said a voice from one of the cubicles.

Nearly dropped dead on the spot.

There was a flushing noise and Gerald emerged, grinning. 'Not feeling too good, then, Dad?'

So relieved it was Gerald in the cubicle I didn't even get cross. I said, 'Gerald, I don't think I have ever looked forward to an event less. My faith is about the size of a pea.'

'That big, eh?'

'What?'

'Well, a pea's bigger than a mustard seed. Hey, Dad, you might even get to move that famous paper-clip at last.'

'Very funny.'

'Besides,' said Gerald, drying his hands at what he always insists on calling the Evangelist Machine ('hot air that takes a long time to produce a rather unsatisfactory result'), 'it can be quite dangerous to walk in victory – look what happened to Lord Nelson.' Patted my shoulder. 'Come on, Dad, you'll be all right.'

It's nice to have your grown-up son encouraging you, but what on earth has Lord Nelson got to do with anything?

Eve Worthington's belief that Brian the bank manager was 'close' didn't appear justified at all. Closer to getting up and walking out than becoming a Christian, if you'd asked me. He was a broad-shouldered man with grizzled grey hair and one of those lined, strong, capable faces that seem to be produced by years of dealing with people and situations on an official basis. Must have been near to retirement age.

When I sat down opposite him, he folded his arms and stared at me with one eyebrow raised, as if to say, 'Go on, then, convert me – if you dare!'

Shook hands and introduced myself nervously as the speaker. Managed to resist a strong temptation to tell him that my account was in perfect order at the moment, and that I would do my very best to ensure that it remained so in the future.

He said, 'So you're the chap who's going to bring us all to our knees, are you? Well, I wish you luck, because you're going to need it.'

He was so resonantly confident that, as the meal went on, my voice almost disappeared altogether, as it usually does when I feel overwhelmed. Not such a bad thing probably, because my bleating protests that I wasn't trying to convert anyone, and my pathetic attempts to engage him in conversation on the subject of banking, about which I know nothing whatsoever, were not worth hearing anyway. He seemed so sure and relaxed and self-contained in his brief answers to my questions, I couldn't imagine him identifying any area of his life that needed the sort of God who was misguided enough to allow himself to be publicly represented by a nerd like me.

(The Oxford English Dictionary, by the way, defines a 'nerd' as a feeble, foolish or uninteresting person, and that's *exactly* how I felt.)

By the time coffee had been served and someone had done an effusive introduction, I was experiencing the strange illusion, known to public speakers everywhere, that ice-cold hands belonging to people who didn't like me were gripping a selection of my internal organs as tightly as possible.

To make matters worse, Eve Worthington, bless her little Christian socks, had positioned herself in such a way that she was able to keep me and Brian the bank manager in view at the same time. She sent an excruciatingly unsubtle wink in my direction, whilst coyly miming her intention to pray throughout my talk by steepling her hands together for a moment in her lap. I resolved to avoid her eye at all costs until I'd finished.

Don't really know why I laid into the Church as heavily as I did when I spoke that evening. Maybe it was the only thing I could do with my confidence so low. It's always simpler to be negative than positive. You can get people laughing more easily when you look at what's wrong with the Church than when you talk about what's right with it.

Whatever the reason, I just know I went on and on about how Christians say silly things, and use silly voices, and sing silly songs, and have silly expectations, and do outreach in silly ways, and read silly books. In fact, on the basis of my talk, there was only one conclusion any outsider could have reached about the Church – it was silly.

One strange and embarrassing thing happened. About halfway through, when I was in full 'silly' flow, I had a sort of thought or feeling or understanding or – oh, I don't know how to describe it. I asked Anne what she thought it was afterwards and she said God was talking to me. I'm glad she said that, because that is what it felt like, but it seems so big-headed to say that God is *talking* to you. Anyway, just to be on the safe side I passed it on to all the people who were there.

I said, 'Look, I could be wrong, but I think God is saying to me that there are some people here tonight who need to forgive God.'

Panicked suddenly at what I could hear coming out of my own mouth. 'Of course,' I went on hastily, 'he can't actually do anything wrong to be forgiven for, but that's what's so difficult sometimes, isn't it? I mean – well, it's not very easy to have a real row with someone who never ever gets anything wrong, is it?' Suddenly seemed to know exactly what to say. 'I mean, there must be some of us who want to climb up onto God's lap like small children and bash at his chest with our little fists, and say, "I hate you! I hate you! I hate you! I asked you to help me and you *didn't* help me. You knew what I was feeling – you *knew* what needed to happen and you didn't do it. You say you love me, but you don't! If you did you would have done something, but you didn't! I hate you!"'

Suddenly spotted Gerald's face, his eyes wide with surprise at what I was saying. Remembered when he was just a little boy.

'When my son was very small,' I said, hoping Gerald wouldn't mind, 'he did exactly that once or twice. First, he'd be really angry, and then when he'd worn himself out with crossness, he'd cry, all curled up on my lap. Then, when he'd cried the last drop of energy away, he'd just fall asleep and I'd hold him for ages. And the important thing is – I think the important thing is that *he had to go through* all that fighting and fretting to get the nasty spiky feelings out of himself, and he did it all in the safest place he knew, which was in my arms.'

Gerald's not the sort of chap whose eyes mist over much, but when I glanced at him I'm pretty sure that's what they were doing.

I looked around at the other faces in the room. 'God doesn't mind you being angry with him,' I said.

*What was I saying?*

'He's used to taking the blame. In fact he'd rather you took it out on him than someone else.' Snatched a breath. 'We'll just spend about five minutes now – those who need to, that is – telling God about the resentment and anger they feel towards him. And anyone who doesn't need to do that can pray for the ones who do.'

Somewhat aghast at what I'd said, and five minutes lasts about three days when a hundred people are made to sit silently in the middle of what was supposed to be a talk. Kept wanting to cut the time down so that people wouldn't get bored or fall asleep or think I was being ridiculous. Five minutes was up at last, thank goodness. Got back into the silly flow, much to the relief of a little group of young teenagers who'd nearly died of containment during the 'Forgiving God' pause.

Could tell from the expression on Eve's face as I finished talking twenty minutes later, that, as far as she was concerned, I had quite definitely not delivered the evangelical goods. And when I risked a glance at Brian the banker, I could understand why she might feel like that. He looked *grim*. As I sat down to a mixture of applause, ranging from a polite patter to enthusiastic hooting from the teenagers, he leaned across the table towards me. Steeled myself to hearing that my overdraft facility was cancelled for all eternity.

He laid a hand on my arm and said, 'Let me help you sell your books.'

I gulped and said, 'All right – thank you.'

Walked over to the book table with him to find Thynn waiting for customers. Introduced Leonard to Brian the bank manager.

'Right, Leonard, my friend,' said Brian, still quite grimly, 'we're going to sell all these books now, and I'm going to need your help. You pass them to me as fast as I flog them, okay?'

Thynn nodded blankly, and said, 'We're going to sell them *all*?'

'No reason why not. Here we go!' Suddenly produced a huge voice that filled the room. 'Excuse me! Everybody look this way, please!'

Never seen anything like it in my life. Brian took a pile of books in his hand and literally sold them by the sheer force of his personality. Every time someone raised a hand to indicate that they wanted a book he flung it across the room to them like a frisbee, shouting, 'Pay at the table! Come on – who's next? Speaker's books! Buy one before they all run out! Thank you, madam – thank you, sir!'

People rather enjoyed it once they got the hang of it. And my self-appointed salesman was right. Every single book we'd

brought got sold. Wonderful! Thynn was in his element, handing books over to Brian as fast as he needed them, while Gerald took money and gave change, and I signed copies for anyone who asked me to. Ended up with the table a sea of notes and coins. There's something very satisfying about lots of money. Maybe there shouldn't be, but there is.

Afterwards, Brian sat at one of the tables with me, sipping at a glass of wine and staring into the distance for a few moments before saying anything. When he did look me straight in the eyes all I could feel was profound fear about what he'd say when he learned that I'd forgotten to fill my cheque stubs in properly, and wouldn't be able to accurately state the balance of my account.

'Wondering why I helped you sell your books, are you?'

'Er . . . well, yes, I suppose so – very grateful, of course . . .'

Brian gazed into the distance again. 'When I was a young man of twenty-one, I was quite into religion – well, Christianity, not just religion. Had been for a good few years. Involved a lot at school and college and so forth. And then, one summer when I was home from college, my kid sister, Millie, who was about ten years younger than me . . .'

The strong face crumpled a little.

'Millie was suddenly taken ill at about tea-time on a Wednesday – and I really mean suddenly. One minute she was right as rain, the next she'd collapsed and been whisked off to the local hospital in an ambulance with some – I dunno – some throat thing. They had to do one of those operations, a tracheotomy it's called, isn't it, actually *in* the ambulance on the way to hospital, although I didn't know that was going on at the time, of course. I just knew she was really bad. I'd heard these awful gasping noises she made as she was carried out to the ambulance, and I was left alone in the house. My mother had followed on in a neighbour's car to be there when the ambulance arrived.'

The resonant voice rumbled with emotion.

'I adored that little sister of mine. Full of life and sunshine, she was. A real innocent – can't have had more than about ten minutes of unhappiness in the whole of her life. Millie. My little sister. I wanted her to live so much. Went upstairs to her bedroom and knelt down among all her silly girly things – things she squeaked and laughed over with her friends, things that meant a lot to her, and I asked God – really *asked* him – to make her better and bring her home again. I wept. Could have sworn he heard me. And I couldn't see how he could refuse anyone who was raging with feeling like I was. I got up in the end, quite calm, and went downstairs to make a cup of tea. I knew it would be all right, you see. God was going to answer my prayer. Then – I'll never forget it, because the kettle began whistling at the precise moment the phone rang. An unforgettable combination. It was my mother on the phone to say that Millie had only lasted ten minutes after she reached the hospital. She must have died more or less the same time that I got up from saying my prayer – my useless prayer. Never did have that particular cup of tea.'

He took another sip of wine.

'After that I wanted nothing to do with God – if he existed. I'd asked him – begged him to save Millie, but he didn't. Why not? No one offered me any answers that sounded halfway reasonable, and I didn't particularly want to hear them anyway. I hated God, and I've gone on hating him ever since in a quiet sort of way.

'Tonight, when you started reading your stuff and going on about all the things that are up the creek with corporate Christianity, it – well, for a start it took me by surprise. I thought you were going to go through all the treacly gentle Jesus stuff, and I'd already decided treacle was just what I didn't want for my fourth course tonight. Your stuff seemed to – how can I describe something that doesn't make more than a ha'p'orth of sense? It seemed to open this narrow little back door that I might even want to squeeze through some time. And then, when you did that bit about forgiving God – look, I've got to ask you this – do you always do that bit? I mean, is it part of the act?'

Shook my head. 'Never done it before. It just – happened. Bit embarrassing actually.'

Brian the bank manager leaned forward and placed his hand on my arm, just as he had done before. 'Don't be embarrassed,' he said very quietly. 'You see – I went home this evening. Suddenly remembered where I live. Stomped in, tried to get cross, wept a bit, and tonight – tonight I'm going to sleep better than I've slept for a very long time.'

Told Gerald and Thynn all about Brian on the way home. Gerald just nodded slowly, stared out of the window and said nothing.

Thynn said, 'Maybe there's a God after all . . .'

## Sunday 20 Feb

Thought about Glander in church today when Edwin was talking about loving your enemies. How can you love someone when you actually want to smash their teeth in? Prayed for him because Jesus said we should.

I said, 'Father, I hate Everett Glander, I really do. I wish he'd stop existing so that I could feel better about myself. You said

62

we've got to pray for our enemies, so I'm going to grit my teeth
and do it now. Whatever I think of Everett, will you meet him
somehow and give him all he needs, and if you've got any spare
miracles hanging about, how about finding a way for me to stop
hating him? Forgive me for being useless. Amen.'

## Monday 21 Feb

Met Anne, Gerald and Thynn in town late afternoon to get
some of those passport-size photographs taken for our big trip.
Hate having my photo taken at the best of times, let alone in those
little booths where you don't get time to comb your hair before
the machine blinds you four times whether you've screwed the
stupid stool to the right height yet or not, then delivers a strip of
pictures showing an alien life-form dressed in your clothes.

We stood in a little bunch waiting nervously for our photographs to come down the slot at the side. Gerald was nearest
when they finally appeared – after about a week. He was most
annoying. Refused to let us even look at them until we were sitting round a table in the Army and Navy restaurant with tea and
doughnuts in front of us. Then he said we had to finish our
doughnuts before handling the pictures because they'd get all
sticky. He may be grown-up, but he can be just as infuriating now
as he ever was. Finally he cleared a space and laid the four strips
out in a row.

Anne said, 'Oh, dear.'

Gerald said, 'Well, all I can say is that I'd certainly think twice
or even three times before letting this little lot into my country if
I was given the choice. Look at the state of us! Mr and Mrs Psychopath and their son Gerald Psychopath, accompanied by The
Creature from the Black Lagoon.'

Gerald was absolutely right. In his strip, Leonard looked like
one of those people in American police dramas who laugh mani-
acally as they're being released on a technicality, and are followed
by Clint Eastwood and shot when they strike again in dark alleys,
Anne's pictures reminded me of the Cabbage Patch dolls that were
all the rage a few years ago (didn't actually tell her that), Gerald

looked like James Dean trying to show emotion whilst under very heavy sedation, and mine bore a dismally striking resemblance to a very sad character called Alfred E. Neuman, who used to appear on the back cover of *Mad* magazine.

Thynn had to go right over the top, as usual, of course. Said my pictures reminded him of the faces of unidentified corpses that have been in the water for a very long time, the ones you sometimes see in touched up photographs in the papers. Charming!

Anne said it didn't really matter because they were only for official documents.

Gerald said, 'I suppose you're right, Mum. But we have to face the fact that if we arrive during daylight hours some immigration official may get very suspicious indeed when he discovers we're not travelling by coffin.'

Changed the subject. Wish I hadn't, because I ended up feeling extremely irritated. Very good example of how my family set out to deliberately annoy me sometimes.

I said, 'Anne, you know I was saying that Percy's roof badly needs repairing?'

(Percy Brain, our ex-actor neighbour is getting very frail now and can hardly walk, let alone climb ladders.)

'Oh, yes,' said Anne.

'Well, this morning, while you were out, I was in our garage looking for one of my tools that seems to have simply ceased to exist – *Gerald* – and I came across those slates left over from when we did our roof, so I thought I'd get the ladder out and put them up.'

'Oh, good, Percy'll be so pleased. He hates the idea of things falling apart around him. So you got it done, did you?'

Shook my head. 'Well, not properly. When I got up there the roof was in a much worse state than I'd realized when I looked at it from the ground. I used what I'd got, but the whole thing needs replacing if you ask me. Wasn't worth bothering really. I only had enough slates to patch one or two holes.'

Anne nodded sympathetically.

Thynn looked dumb.

Gerald said, 'A futile gesture in fact.'

Now, why, I have asked myself all day since that moment, did Anne and Leonard, and Gerald himself, fall about laughing at that comment? Why? Are all three of them mad? I asked them to tell me what was so funny but they downright refused. Said if I thought about it I'd see what had made them laugh. Well, I've thought – and I can't!

A FUTILE GESTURE IN FACT

There it is – this great joke of theirs. They keep saying it and then sniggering. Why, when it's not funny? I tried to mend Percy's roof with my bits of slate, and Gerald said it was a futile gesture.

WHY IS THAT FUNNY?

If one of them doesn't tell me soon I shall tie up all my special belongings in a little spotted handkerchief on the end of a pole and leave home – I shall really.

## Tuesday 22 Feb

Funny how worrying things line up like horses in a race, isn't it? The leader, and odds-on favourite in the Adrian Plass Handicap is Vlad's Children's Talk, closely followed by Everett Glander's Existence, with What's Funny About A Futile Gesture coming up on the rails, and the outsider, Gerald's Future, biding its time at the back in fourth place.

## Wednesday 23 Feb

My support group here tonight to pray about the weekend, when Anne, Gerald, Leonard and I are going to Scotland to do two meetings.

Support group has grown a bit since our first meeting. Tonight there was Edwin Burlesford, Stephanie Widgeon, a thin middle-aged lady with bright, blank eyes who moved to the area a few months ago, Leonard Thynn, Gloria Marsh, Richard and Doreen Cook and, of course, Anne and Gerald.

Looked round at them all as they sat in our sitting-room. They're a good crowd, but very sort of – real. Couldn't help wishing I was surrounded by mature, wise-faced, spiritual giants radiating quiet but powerful blessing in my direction as I bravely prepared to pour myself out for others. I'm sure Billy Graham doesn't have anyone in his group remotely like Leonard Thynn who, tonight, was wearing a pair of those trick spectacles with the eyeballs that fall out on a spring when you lean forward. Why? I mean – why?

Thynn really annoys me sometimes. Tonight, as part of my 'Reporting Back' I started to tell everyone about a conversation I had in Derby with a lady who came up to speak to me after the meeting. Rather looking forward to talking about this particular encounter because it was a bit like something out of one of those testimony books. Was planning to tell the story in a way that would show how wonderful I'd been, then finish by making it clear that it was God who'd done the work really. That way, you get to boast and be humble at the same time. Thynn ruined it.

Really tried to build up the tension. I said, 'The poor woman was in tears before I spoke to her, but when she'd finished listening to what I had to say, she quite suddenly lit up, and – '

'Smoker, was she?'

Short pause while everyone turned to Thynn.

I said, 'Pardon, Leonard?'

He looked puzzled and said, 'Sorry, only you said she suddenly lit up, so I assumed she must've been a smoker. What? *What?*'

Gerald enjoyed this enormously, of course. Story ruined.

As we came up to prayer time I confessed that I was feeling quite nervous about these two meetings up north, and asked the group to specially pray that I would hear the Lord's voice clearly in my preparation. Stephanie Widgeon, whom I've never spoken to very much, and who was here for the first time tonight, leaned towards me nodding and smiling significantly, and said, 'Adrian, has it ever occurred to you that the Church is not just a building made of bricks and mortar?'

I said, 'Yes, it has. Why?'

'I think it's the people, don't you?'

'Yes.'

Waited for a punch-line, but there wasn't one. Stephanie sat back in her chair, shaking her head in wonder, and biting her bottom lip as if to contain the ecstasy she'd experienced in passing on this shattering revelation. She obviously felt some great spiritual moment had occurred. Perhaps it had. Everyone else looked rather blank. Odd . . .

Prayer time disrupted at first by the arrival of Norma Twill, who'd come round to leave something for Anne. She put her head round the door just after everyone had lowered their eyes. Wouldn't have mattered at all except that stupid Thynn, who was sitting facing the door, raised his head just as she walked in, and she screamed loudly on seeing his eyeballs apparently hanging out of their sockets.

Why . . . ?

Was going to go out and comfort poor Norma, but Anne caught hold of the elastic waistband at the back of my Y-fronts under my tee-shirt and catapulted me back into my seat.

Quite a good time of prayer once we got settled again. Lovely to feel all these people caring about what happens to me. Prayed about Scotland, of course, and a meeting on March fourth that Richard has promised to drive me to. Asked if anyone had anything from the Lord about the children's talk, but no one had this time either.

Prayer time slightly spoiled by a rather disturbing prayer from Doreen Cook towards the end. I don't know what's the matter with her at the moment.

She said, 'Lord, we just want to ask that when Adrian – frail, weak, inadequate, incompetent and totally lacking in strength and talent as the world judges such things – stands up before those rows and rows of intimidating, judgmental, critical faces, his stomach turning to water, feeling that his trembling legs will never support him for long enough to deliver his unworthy message – that when he stands up there, Lord, he'll forget the ever-present possibility that his listeners will heckle, throw fruit, shout derisively and eventually jeer him off the stage and possibly pursue him with a view to committing physical violence on his person. Let him feel encouraged, Lord, by the knowledge that even though he may experience the lurching nausea of fear, the misery of abject humiliation and the searing pain of a steel toe-cap in the side of his head, it matters not as long as one person has found some small encouragement from his words. Yea, though he be systematically battered to death with half-bricks and lengths of lead piping, let him rejoice and be glad! Amen.'

Gerald murmured in my ear, 'Bet you can't wait for the weekend, Dad.'

Suddenly realized from the concentrated, straining expression on Richard Cook's face that he was either trying to control indigestion or about to have a 'picture'. Gerald said afterwards that he would have preferred the indigestion.

'God has given me a picture,' said Richard, in the peculiar, declamatory voice he adopts on such occasions. 'I see, as it were, a great multitude of folks of all ages on a hill, and behold they are singing and full of great joy concerning one who has brought them much refreshment ...'

'It's either Graham Kendrick leading a Make Way march or a Coca-Cola advert,' whispered Gerald.

'And behold I see the one who has brought this joy, and his name – his name is – Gordon Stillsby.'

Short puzzled pause.

'Gordon Stillsby?' echoed Gloria Marsh at last, looking up in surprise. 'Who's Gordon Stillsby? I thought you were going to say his name was Adrian Plass. I don't know anyone called Gordon Stillsby. There's no one called Gordon Stillsby at church, is there Edwin? Gordon Stillsby ...'

Prayer time degenerated after that into a discussion about who the mysterious Gordon Stillsby might be. Richard claimed he'd never heard of the name until it was vouchsafed to him just now, and Doreen wondered if Gordon Stillsby might be my spiritual name (whatever that might mean), and that perhaps I ought to call myself Gordon Stillsby when I was ministering publicly. Anne reduced to near hysterics by this, and we all ended up laughing, thank goodness. Edwin suggested gently that Richard might have got a bit carried away, and Richard agreed that it could be possible because Satan does seek to deceive even the elect. I hoped that would be that, and it was, except that Gerald annoyingly insisted on calling me Gordon for the rest of the evening.

Wish I could find a way to avoid blushing at the worst possible times. Very embarrassing moment as everyone was leaving. Gloria Marsh, who is, I suppose, from a purely objective point of view, attractively constructed, has never been anything but a sister in the Lord to me, despite silly comments and pointed remarks from Gerald and Anne respectively in the past. She was the last to leave and stood *very* close to me in the doorway. After saying goodbye, she added, 'I wanted to say, Adrian, that if you ever needed me to do a spot of warming up one evening, I'd be more than happy to share from the front.'

Felt my face turning bright purple and let out a ridiculous little bleating laugh. Why couldn't I have just said, 'Thank you very much, I'll certainly bear that in mind'? Anne and Gerald both saw my face burning. Very aware of them staring at my back as I closed the door behind Gloria. Anne didn't say anything afterwards. Just raised one eyebrow in a perhaps-it's-about-time-we-thought-about-having-single-beds sort of way.

After Anne had gone to bed, Gerald said, 'I've been thinking, Gordon.'

I said, '*Don't* call me Gordon – what about?'

'Well, you know Let God Spring into Royal Acts of Harvest Growth?'

'The Christian festival, yes.'

'And you know Gloria?'

'Ye-e-es.'

'Well, if Gloria ever – you know – shared from the front at Let God Spring into Royal Acts of Harvest Growth . . .'

Sighed heavily. 'Do get on with it, Gerald.'

'Well, I know where she'd have to do it.'

'And where might that be?'

'The Big Top.'

I said, 'Gerald, that joke is shallow, sexist and completely unfunny.'

He said, 'Sorry, Gordon.'

## Thursday 24 Feb

Out for a drink with Gerald early evening to give Anne a chance to finish off the packing for Scotland. After getting our second pints, I spoke to him as casually as I could.

'So, how do you see the future?'

'How do I see the future?'

'Yes.'

'You really want to know how I see the future?'

'Yes.'

'All right, well, I suppose I see the future as a really very extensive period of time, beginning on the front edge of the present, and not a very great distance from the past. I guess there's a good case for assuming that each moment of the future, will, in its turn, become the present, and that those moments of present will, in *their* turn, eventually combine to constitute the past. So, how do *you* see the future?'

Realized I was wasting my time.

Gerald's Future has worked its way into third place, and the odds become shorter with every passing day.

## Friday 25 Feb

Writing this in the car on the way to Scotland.

Away very early this morning with Anne, Gerald and Thynn. Love these early starts. Planning to stay somewhere tonight and do the last bit to our hotel near Edinburgh tomorrow. Gerald, who wasn't aware of this very simple, sensible plan, laughed and said that, as long as he drove and I didn't we'd easily reach our destination tonight.

Bit annoyed really. Asked him what was wrong with my driving.

He said, 'Well, not a lot, if you leave aside little things like your tendency to change down a gear when you come to bends on the motorway.'

Absolute rubbish! I am not a slow driver. I have just said to him that if he gets us to our hotel by six o'clock I will do ten press-ups and sing 'Three Blind Mice' in the hotel foyer immediately we arrive.

Totally confident that six o'clock is an impossible target.

*6:15 p.m.*

I am inexpressibly relieved that we are only staying in this hotel for one night. I shall not emerge from my room again until we leave.

## Saturday 26 Feb

Really good meeting tonight. People came into the hall smiling, and went on smiling and laughing right the way through. Unfortunately a lot of them also laughed through all the moving bits. Still, never mind, I'm used to that, and it all made for a very warm time.

Had to rescue a customer from Thynn afterwards. Leonard was helping to sell copies of my books, and had just been approached by an elderly person as I arrived at the back of the hall.

'Are any of Adrian's books suitable,' the doddery white-haired man was asking, 'for a middle-aged nurse living in Hong Kong, who used to be a keen Christian and is just getting interested again, was divorced a year ago, is a passionate basketball fan and has an irrational but deep-rooted fear of pre-war Bakelite products?'

Stupid Thynn simply collected together my three books, held them out and said, 'Yes, Adrian wrote all these three specially with people like that in mind. That'll be fourteen pounds and ninety-seven pence, please.'

Rescued the man from Thynn's outrageous sales techniques.

Pre-war Bakelite products?

Stayed in a boarding house where the staff do not regard me as a very sad person indeed.

## Sunday 27 Feb

Day off after going to the local church this morning.

Wonderful time exploring and relaxing. Staying tonight and tomorrow in a holiday cottage high up on a hill, kindly lent to us (the cottage, not the hill) by a local church member. Beautiful situation.

We're all sleeping in a row in a sort of dormitory bedroom reached by climbing an outside stairway made of wood. Should be a very comfortable place to spend the night, except that if you want to use the toilet you have to unbolt the bedroom door, go down the outside steps, unlock the front door of the cottage, use the toilet, lock the front door behind you again, climb the stairway, go back into the bedroom and bolt the door behind you. Gerald suggested just now that we use a bucket that's obviously been put up here for the purpose, but – well, it's one of those echoing, metal buckets and I just – couldn't. Made sure I went to the toilet before going to bed.

Too tired to write any more tonight.

## Monday 28 Feb

*11:45 p.m.*

Back in the cottage at last after the final event of our little tour. Can hardly write about the events of last night without all the feelings of panic and fear coming back.

Should have been a good, peaceful night up here in our dormitory.

Dropped off quite quickly after writing my diary, but was awakened in the early hours by a voice in the distance calling, 'Help! Help! Help me!'

Said a quick prayer asking for God's protection and leaned over to the next bed to wake Anne up. Found she wasn't there! Suddenly realized it must be Anne calling for help. Threw my dressing gown on and headed for the door at top speed. Wish I'd known what had happened to Anne before going through that door.

Later, Anne told me that she'd woken up at about two in the morning and decided to go down the steps and into the house to use the toilet, but she forgot to turn on the outside light before leaving the bedroom. Setting off down the wooden stairway in the dark, she also forgot that the steps turned to the left halfway down, and walked straight over the edge, falling about six feet onto the stony ground below.

I forgot to turn the outside light on too. Only difference between Anne's experience and mine was that I *sprinted* down the steps forgetting that they turned to the left. Didn't just fall. I took off, a bit like a ski-jumper. Landed some way beyond Anne, who must have been deeply alarmed when a shadowy, Eddie Edwards-like figure launched itself into space above her head.

Ended up both crawling around in the dark moaning and groaning with pain. Learned later that Gerald and Thynn heard our wretched cries coming from what sounded like a long way away and thought there might be an axe-murderer or something on the loose – so they locked the door! Didn't bother to check our beds first. Cheers!

Found our way into the house eventually and gave each other first aid. Dozed for the rest of the night.

Had to go up on stage for my meeting tonight covered in plasters, bruises and bandages to talk about my victorious walk with

Christ. Noticed that people found the account of how I got my injuries much funnier than anything else I said. Rather annoyed at first, but realized, talking to people afterwards, that telling stories against yourself has a rather charming, self-effacing effect. Anne's right – I'll keep it in.

Caught up by a letter marked URGENT from Stephanie Widgeon today. In it she said that it had been revealed to her that the Church was actually the people and not the building, and she thought I ought to know immediately. Funny, I thought she said that in the support meeting. Odd . . .

Home tomorrow!

## Tuesday 1 March

Why is the world of long-distance road travelling so obsessed with breakfasts? In one of the places we stopped at on the way home they did the 'All Day Fill-em-up Farmhouse' breakfast, the 'American Big-boy Texas Tummy Tempter' breakfast, the 'Super Gi-normous Three-meals-in-one' breakfast, the 'Bigger Than Any Breakfast You Ever Saw In Your Life Belly Buster' breakfast, and the 'Pile On A Platter For A Peckish Pachyderm' breakfast.

Asked for a small piece of dry toast and a weak tea.

The waitress, who can't have been much more than twelve and a half, said dispassionately, 'You mean, you want one of our "Sunshine Raft On The Old Mississippi" breakfasts.'

'I don't care what you call it,' I replied, 'as long as I'm not paying for the name.'

Arrived home late tonight. All a bit ratty. Not surprising after getting hardly any sleep the night before last. Axe-murderer on the loose! I ask you . . .

Still, generally, the trip went well. Thynn nearly drove us mad inventing bad Scottish jokes all the way down. Told him that if he carries on doing it now that we're back I shall donate his body to medical research before he dies. Some horrible examples:

Q. What does a Scottish owl do?
A. Hoots mon.

Q. What does a Scottish boxer call the fighters he trains with?
A. Sporran partners.

Q. What do you call a cockney who's looking down a rabbit hole?
A. Edinburgh.

Q. What's the difference between a kitchen appliance used for rapidly stirring a combination of foods, and a bottle of Scotch whisky?
A. One's a Food Mixer, and the other's a Mood Fixer.

Men have been killed for less.

## Wednesday 2 March

Sle-e-e-e-e-e-e-e-e-e-e-e-e-e-e-e-e-e-e-e-e-e-e-e-e-e-p.

## Thursday 3 March

Quite a lot of people send us their family newsletters, and some of them are fine, but when they're like the one that arrived this morning I feel really intimidated. Showed it to Gerald, who made being-sick noises when he'd finished it.

Dearest _____ (Please fill in own name),

It hardly seems possible that a whole year has passed since our last newsletter went out. What a lot has happened since then! Each of us has seen change, beginning with the youngest.

### Naomi (age 5)

Little Naomi has become more spiritually alive than ever during the last twelve months. All four of us have the stigmata now. She is also very bright, but Rebecca and I are anxious that she should not be pushed too far, too quickly, where school work is concerned. She must certainly finish her reception year before taking maths 'A' level, and there is absolutely no question of her undertaking piano recitals in Europe until she has passed her seventh birthday.

Naomi continues to work hard at building up the Christian Union that she started at her junior school last term, and is very encouraged by a recent experience of personally leading her orthodox Jewish headmaster and several other members of staff (including the caretaker and three dinner-ladies) to Christ.

Naomi's after-school activities include a chess class on Monday (she earns her own pocket money by teaching that), applied thermonuclear dynamics on Tuesday, netball training with other members of the County team on Thursdays, and a soup-run into the East End every Friday evening. Typically, Naomi taught herself judo and karate to black-belt standard from textbooks before embarking on this potentially dangerous occupation.

Naomi is easily the most popular girl in her class, and was voted Miss Young and Humble at church this year, although she refused to accept the trophy saying that she was an unworthy winner. This act of pure unselfishness resulted in her being nominated for the award of Most Humble Church Member of All, an award which she subsequently won and decided to accept, feeling that it would have been uncharitable, churlish, and subtly vain to refuse.

Please pray with Rebecca and I that Naomi will learn how to put herself first from time to time. Failure to do this is her major fault.

### Joshua (age 16)

Joshua has gained fifteen A grade GCSEs and nine spiritual gifts this year, including Sociology and Prophecy (the one to be most earnestly sought after, according to the apostle Paul – prophecy, that is, not sociology). Over the next two years he hopes to take the Word of the Lord to Communist China, and twelve 'A' levels.

Joshua spent his summer holiday converting Guatemala with a group of pals, constructing a life-size working model of Apollo 3 out of drinking straws, and practising the five Cantonese dialects in which he is now practically fluent.

It is not all plain sailing with Joshua, however. A typically wayward and rebellious sixteen-year-old, he has several times sneaked off to his room to do a couple of hours extra academic study when he knows he should be concentrating on tightening up his dressage skills in the back paddock ready for the Olympics, and on more than one occasion he has actually disappeared from the house altogether, only to be discovered guiltily shopping for the elderly lady who lives two doors away from us, or sitting and reading to her for long periods after cooking and serving her evening meal. When Rebecca and I gently pointed out that we can't always do exactly what we want, Joshua asked our forgiveness and repointed the brickwork of every house in the street as an act of repentance. Rebecca and I feel sure he'll come through in the end.

Both Oxford and Cambridge Universities have applied to have Joshua join them in two years' time, and he will probably fly up (as soon as his pilot's licence comes through) to look over both establishments before making a decision. Please pray for Joshua's feelings of inadequacy as he prepares to deal with fellow-students and their inevitable dependency on him during this next sixth-form phase of his life.

*Rebecca*

Rebecca continues to enjoy producing home-made jam, bread, cakes, wine, preserves, crocheted bedspreads, small animal models made out of baked dough, dried flower decorations, knitted baby-clothes, banners and kneeling mats for our local church, and meals for the housebound.

She has completed her first novel this year, held a successful one-woman oil-painting exhibition, been awarded a third Open University degree, and continues to single-handedly look after our twelve-acre ornamental garden, when her duties as mother, wife, amateur apiarist, semi-professional photographer, local magistrate, prison visitor, hospital volunteer, leading light in the amateur dramatic association, treasurer of the ladies tennis club, district council member and world chairperson of Women Against Poverty allow.

Rebecca is currently looking for some new challenge to occupy the spare time that she, in common with many non-working mothers, finds hanging so heavily on her hands. Next year, in addition to her present activities, she plans to become a special policewoman, stand as a prospective parliamentary candidate, complete a solo sailing trip around the world, and find a method of bottling gooseberries that doesn't lose all the flavour.

Please pray that Rebecca will develop a stronger sense of self-worth in the company of other women.

### Simon

Simon has spent much of this year seeking the Lord's will for his life, and longing to serve in some more specific way. There has, however, been little space for this prayer to be answered as Simon's time has been filled with distractions throughout the twelve months, not least of which was the leading of twenty-five convoys of thirty lorries each to mid-European countries in need of aid. This took up most of the summer.

It did seem possible that the autumn would be free for Simon to concentrate on seeking guidance, but flying back from what had been an amazingly successful business trip in Hong Kong, his plane crashed into the Pacific Ocean and Simon, who was the sole survivor, swam ashore to an island inhabited by primitive natives who had never heard the Gospel before. In the two months that Simon was stranded on the island he managed to learn the native tongue, devise a written version of the language, and translate a large part of the New Testament (memorized) into a form that the islanders could understand. The entire population of the island became Christians as a result, and many of them set out in canoes to take the good news to thousands of other primitive peoples living on islands in that part of the Pacific.

Simon was eventually rescued by a passing ship which was named *The Dirty Digger* when it landed at the island, but had been rechristened *Redeemed* by the time it arrived at Portsmouth. Simon arrived home in the new year, frustrated by these delays, but as determined as ever to see if the Lord had some task that might be specially his.

In February he went into retreat in a monastery in Wales, and was just beginning to feel that he was getting somewhere, when, one night, the building caught fire, and Simon rescued twenty-two monks whose vows of silence had prevented them from calling for help.

Simon stayed in Wales with the monks for several weeks after the fire, helping to rebuild the monastery and telling the brothers about the new life of the Spirit that was promised to all Christians. All twenty-two made fresh commitments as a result, and the Prior pledged that he would spread the good news throughout the world-wide order of which they were part.

Simon therefore returned without the leading he had sought, and is hoping that next year might be the time when the Lord sees fit to give him a substantial task.

Pray that Simon will find the strength to ignore distractions from the evil one when they appear, and run for the finishing line in a more decisive and intelligent way.

That's all now from this very ordinary Christian family. See you next year!

Yours,

Simon, Rebecca, Joshua and Naomi.

P.S. We usually add a little bit at the bottom in Biro to make it more personal, but our time is the Lord's, not ours – if you see what we mean.

I think a firing squad would be the answer ...

## Friday 4 March

Odd day today. Started badly and ended well.

The bad start was when, feeling a bit intimidated by the heroic exploits of Simon, Joshua, Rebecca and Naomi, I woke up determined to put into practice something I read in a magazine article last night about 'Praise Offered As Sacrifice'. The writer of the article said that we should be especially willing to give praise and worship to God at times when we don't feel like doing it. If we made this sacrifice, the article explained, God would reward us by turning our act of will into a veritable hymn of spontaneous joy that would bless us and all those around us.

Started as soon as I woke, feeling, as usual, like a dead slug, by saying 'Praise the Lord!' four or five times as I lay staring at the ceiling. Felt a bit strange and I sounded a bit croaky, but the article did say that one had to persist until one came through into the place of transfiguration. Occurred to me that if I got through a lot of praise very quickly the speed of 'coming through' might be concertinaed, as it were.

Said, 'Praise the Lord! Hallelujah! Amen!' very rapidly and repeatedly as I got out of bed and put my dressing gown on. Caught a glimpse of Anne's face peering over the bedclothes as I went out of the room. Her eyes were wild and staring. Continued praising by an act of the will all the way along the landing and into the bathroom. Carried on all through my shower and while I was in the lavatory. Flagging a bit by the time I made the return trip along the landing, but still managed to emit the odd 'Praise the Lord'.

No sign at breakfast that my act of will had been transformed into a hymn of joy that would bless me and all those around me. On the contrary – those around me (Anne and Gerald) looked more morose and unhappy and unblessed than usual.

Asked what was wrong.

Anne rubbed her eyes and said wearily, 'Adrian, I don't know what hare-brained scheme you're pursuing at the moment, and, to be honest, I don't really care. What I do care about is the way it affects me. I want to make it very clear that I don't appreciate being woken – early – out of what *was* a beautiful sleep by a religious maniac who is incapable of keeping his wretched outpourings to himself.'

'Wretched outpourings? I can't believe you're calling – '

'It really does puzzle me that, after all these years, and knowing what you know about the sheer – the sheer *sanity* of God, that you go on being sucked in by these half-baked twits who can't relax until they've got other people behaving in the same bizarre fashion as themselves.'

'I'll have you know,' I said with dignity, 'that this particular "half-baked twit" as you so uncharitably call him, has one of the most respected ministries in this country. More than twenty fellowships come under his umbrella.'

Anne said, 'Well, I hope the weather keeps fine for them.'

'That's not funny,' I said.

'Yes, it is!' cackled Gerald.

Really made me cross. 'And what about you, Gerald – have you got something serious to say about this morning? Or are you just going to make a joke of it as usual?'

Gerald shrugged. 'Well, I didn't have to suffer the awful awakening that Mum did, but I heard just about everything else after that. It was pretty awful, Dad. It sounded as though a Pentecostal convention was being held in our bathroom with a fringe praise-meeting going on in the loo. Then I heard you still muttering stuff along the landing on your way back to your room. It *was* a bit wearing.'

'I see. A bit wearing. And presumably you would agree with your mother's restrained description of my sacrifice of praise as the "wretched outpourings of a religious maniac", would you?'

'Oh, no,' said Gerald, 'I don't think I'd describe it like that. No – when I was listening to you in the bathroom and the toilet this morning it reminded me of something else, but I couldn't quite put my finger on what it was.' He paused and thought for a moment. 'Ah, yes, that's it! I know what it was. I think I'd describe it as a sort of – spiritual flatulence. Morning was breaking.'

Too angry to speak. Went up and shut myself in my study until they'd both gone out. Hoped that as the day went by they'd start to feel guilty and ashamed about the way they'd spoken to me. I planned to be hurt and not easily consoled, but eventually forgive them.

Had to leave for my evening speaking engagement before Anne and Gerald came home. Richard Cook had offered to drive me in our car so that I'd be fresh for the meeting when I got there. Set off about half past four.

Sometimes wish Richard's sense of humour was just a little more highly developed. We turned into a nearby garage to get some petrol, and just as we were approaching the pumps, Richard said, 'Is the petrol cap on your side?'

I said, 'Well, it's always been very supportive.'

He said, 'No, I mean – which side of the car is the petrol cap?'

Richard dropped me off at Wopsley Community Fellowship Church at about six-thirty before driving away to visit an aunt who lived locally.

First time I'd ever been to this church. Felt a bit lonely and isolated, especially after what had happened with Anne and Gerald in the morning. Had a bad attack of the 'What-on-earth-is-a-person-like-me-doing-here?' jitters. What would these trusting people say if they knew that their guest speaker was still in the middle of a giant sulk with his wife and son? Wished Anne and Gerald were there so that we could all say sorry and hug each other and make everything all right.

Talk went all right, I suppose, then afterwards coffee and cakes were served so that people could 'chat' while they circulated. Must say it was a very warm, friendly, relaxed atmosphere. Looked around the church for the first time (I never notice anything until after I've spoken) and saw that it was very plain except for a large, highly complex but very crudely carved wooden cross on the wall above the shallow stage at the front. Commented on it to an elderly lady carrying a tray of coffee around.

She said cheerfully, 'Ah, yes, that's our cross. We don't like that at all.'

She moved on with her tray before I could ask her what she meant.

Pointed out the cross a little later to a youngish man who was busy stacking chairs to make room for people to 'circulate'.

I said, 'That's a fine cross you have up there.'

He stopped for a moment, wiped his forehead and looked quite surprised. 'Do you really like it? We think it's hideous. Just the place for it, though, up in front there, don't you think?'

'Yes, but why – '

He'd gone.

Finally nobbled Daniel Bisset, the elder-in-charge, a large, happy man, who seemed to be everybody's friend, and asked him about the cross.

'Ah, yes!' Daniel nodded and beamed. 'We're very proud of that ugly old cross, we really are. You see, we always said we'd never have such things here. Had a special meeting, we did, eleven or twelve years ago when we got started, and the whole caboodle of us agreed that we didn't want any such stuff cluttering up the place. That's why it's so good to see it up there now – makes it even more important, if you see what I mean.'

I said, 'No, I'm sorry, I don't see what you mean at all. Everyone I talk to about that cross tells me how much you don't want it here, and in the same breath they tell me how proud you all are of it. I don't understand at all.'

Daniel guffawed loudly. 'See what you mean, see what you mean – okay, I'll tell you what happened. It's all about this old chap called Eric Carter – lived on his own up in one of those slummy cottages that used to be where the back of Sainsbury's is now. Eric was in his – ooh, his mid-seventies when I first met him, couldn't see too well and he was a real old pagan, according to his own estimate. We met him when some of the harvest stuff got taken round his house one Monday after the service, and whoever it was went round left a list of things going on at the church. Well, Eric was a wary old devil, and a bit crabby at first, but he was lonely, so he did turn up at one of our social evenings that we do, and he seemed to have a good time. After that – I dunno, one thing led to another – I saw him round at his home quite a bit as well as him coming to the odd service, and the long and the short of it is that, in the end, he became a Christian. Knelt down like a baby one evening up there at the front and said he wanted to give his life to Jesus.'

'And the cross?'

'One day, when I was round visiting him, Eric suddenly says, "Would it be all right if I said a word or two at the front next Sunday, and can someone pick me up and bring me down?" Well, I was a bit surprised at this because Eric always prided himself on making his own way down to the church whenever he came, but there was no way he was going to tell me what he was on about, so I just agreed to do what he'd asked and that was that.

'The next Sunday, Eric arrives at the church – can't remember who picked him up – and he actually walked into the building pushing the wheelbarrow that we keep in the shed round the back. And lying across the top of this wheelbarrow, not in it because it was too big, was this mystery object wrapped up in sacks and whatnot. Well, you can imagine, by the time Eric got up to do his turn everyone was agog. What *was* he going to say, and

84

what was that *thing* in the wheelbarrow standing next to him? And then old Eric started to say his piece . . .'

Daniel paused for a moment, his eyes bright with the memory.

'Eric talked about how lonely he'd been before he started coming down to church do's, as he called them, and how surprised he'd been at the friendliness, not just towards him, but among the rest of us. He said how he'd been taught as a kid that you keep yourself to yourself in church so as not to interfere with anyone else, and he'd been afraid it was going to be like that. I can still remember what he said.

'"You all seemed to be lookin' after each other," those were his words, "an' makin' sure each other was 'appy. It made me want to be in it. An' now I am. I didn't know it was Jesus doin' it, but I do now."

'And then he got a bit pink and said he'd made something for the church to thank us for being nice to each other and to him, so that he ended up meeting Jesus. He got one of the lads to come and help him unwrap the thing on the wheelbarrow and hold it up, and, of course, it was that cross that's up the front there now. It would be a sort of sign, he said, of how friendly Jesus wants us to be. Turned out he'd worked on it for weeks in the little shed at the back of his cottage, but, what with poor lighting and him having not very good eyesight anyway, the thing was all over the place, and some of it a very strange shape, as you can see.'

'But you put it up.'

'Course we did! That cross comes down over my dead body. It tells us and anyone else who bothers to find out that a man came to Jesus because we were nice to each other. We don't like crosses, but we like *that* cross.'

I glanced around. 'Is Eric here tonight?'

'Probably,' said Daniel with sudden gentleness, 'but you won't see him if he is. He died about four years ago – gone to put in a good word for us I hope.'

Richard arrived soon after that to take me home. Said he'd had a time of splitting and stacking at his aunt's house. Thought he was talking about some obscure area of dialectical religious philosophy until he explained that he'd been chopping firewood for her.

Both sat in silence for some time on the way back. Then Richard suddenly said, 'Ha! Always been very supportive – ha!'

Better late than never, I suppose.

Looking forward all the way home to telling Anne about my conversation with Daniel Bisset. Remembered, just as I walked into the kitchen where Anne and Gerald were sitting over coffee, that I was still in the middle of sulking and being deeply hurt about the reaction to my sacrifice of praise. Had about two seconds to decide whether to be nice or not . . .

I wonder if Eric Carter knows that his ugly old cross was still doing its work in our kitchen four years after he'd gone?

Anne and I away until Sunday night for a supposed-to-be-romantic-but-usually-begins-with-a-big-row-and-then-gets-a-lot-better-after-that-if-not-actually-romantic weekend. Anne says if I record a single word of it in here she's going to write a book about what happened on our wedding night.

## Monday 7 March

Wonderful weekend. (I'm allowed to say that.)

I am absolutely determined to take this children's talk thing by the scruff of the neck and deal with it! I have been so *weak*. Every time I decide to do something about it I chicken out. Not this time! I'm going to phone Reverend Spool tonight when I get back from work and tell him I'm not doing it. What a relief!

*11:00 p.m.*

Chickened out. Do it tomorrow.

## Tuesday 8 March

Chickened out.

## Wednesday 9 March

Cluck, cluck!

## Thursday 10 March

Laid egg.

## Friday 11 March

Couldn't help moaning and groaning about the blasted children's talk while we were all watching television in the living-room tonight. Anne got really cross. Told me to either do something or shut up about it for ever.

Went through to the kitchen and, after a few minutes, found the courage to ring Reverend Spool. As soon as he heard who it was he said, 'Ah, Adrian, I cannot express to you in words the pleasurable anticipation that all of us are feeling about your visit to our church on Sunday. Quite a number of folk who are not regular attenders are making a special trip from a very great distance to be here for the occasion. I am quite sure that I would not be misrepresenting the general excitement if I were to say that, for many, it will be a high spot – if not *the* high spot – of our year here at St Dermot's. We are so *very* grateful to you for sparing us the time from your busy schedule!'

Couldn't very well say, 'Well, tough cheese, Vladimir, because I'm not coming', could I?

Told him I'd just rung to say how much I was looking forward to it, and how terrific it was of him to ask me. Felt like someone on Death Row having a good old chinwag with the electrician.

Went back into the living-room.

Gerald took one look at my face, and said, 'Get the Paxo out, Mum.'

## Saturday 12 March

Really tried hard to feel ill this morning. Lay in bed for a long time straining to detect a problem in some part of my body. Nothing beyond a slight twinge in the left elbow. Went into the bathroom and made vague retching noises, hoping that Anne would hear and suggest I went back to bed.

Oh, the sweet, sweet fantasy of hearing her voice speaking to the vicar on the phone and apologizing on my behalf because I'm too sick to do the children's talk.

Staggered downstairs, leaning on walls and doorposts as I went, trying to look white and drawn. Almost believed in my sickness myself by now. Arrived in the kitchen at last, finishing with what I thought was a rather stylish little lurch from the doorway to a chair at the table where Anne and Gerald were eating breakfast.

Said in a hollow, sickening-for-something voice, 'Anne, I really don't feel all that good.'

Didn't even look up. She said, 'Well, stay in and keep warm, then, because you've got that children's talk tomorrow.'

How could she be so heartless?

'Anne,' I said, 'you don't seem to understand. I thought I was going to be sick upstairs just now.'

Gerald turned the page of his newspaper and said, 'Changed your mind, did you?'

I said, 'Are you suggesting that I was putting it on?'

'I don't know, but you certainly weren't throwing it up. Face it, Dad, thespian flu isn't going to get you anywhere. To get any sympathy from us you'll have to be actually in the process of being torn to pieces by wild dogs and on the absolute point of death. And even then one of us will ask the dogs to stop for a moment while we pass you the phone so that with your last breath you can tell the vicar you're not coming.'

Went and played a round of golf. No danger of compassion fatigue in my family.

## Sunday 13 March

Woke at six-thirty with the thought of this blasted children's talk dragging my spirits down like a great lead weight. How could I have been so *incredibly* stupid? Made one last frantic effort to get Anne to phone them and say I was sick and she'd come and do it instead, but she got all hung up on trivial issues like 'truth' and 'keeping your promises' and 'learning through your own mistakes'.

Gerald said he'd come along to offer moral support. Accepted his offer just for the company. Slightly disturbed, however, when, just as we were about to leave, he shouted, 'Joyce Grenfell and I are off now, Mum.' Realized I was about to provide enough ammunition to last him a very long time.

As we walked through the door of St Dermot's at nine-fifteen, Gerald said, 'Bet you a bottle of claret you tell at least three lies in the next five minutes, Dad.'

I said, 'Don't be absurd, Gerald.'

The Reverend Spool, who, Gerald reckons, is the most vicar-ish vicar who ever vicared, hurried over when he saw us come in, clasped my hand earnestly in both of his, and said, 'I cannot tell you how grateful we all are to you for agreeing to come, Adrian. I expect the last thing you want is yet another speaking engagement on top of all the others.'

I replied, 'No, no, it's a pleasure to be here, it really is.'

Just behind my left ear Gerald whispered, 'One.'

'But, of course,' went on Spool, 'this is slightly different, is it not? Today you will be addressing our little ones.' He twinkled away appropriately. 'Something of a novelty for you, I dare say.'

'Yes,' I said, 'but I've been looking forward to it enormously, I really have.'

'Two and a half,' murmured Gerald from behind my right ear.

'By the way, you will let us know your normal fee for such a talk, won't you?' Spool was still unwinding. 'We shall need to alert Mr Frobisher, our treasurer. We naturally insist on paying whatever sum you usually charge.'

He really meant it. Suddenly wanted to appear as generous as he was.

'I don't think we'll bother about that on this occasion,' I said, hoping he'd sense how great a sacrifice I was making. 'To be honest, money has never been very near the top of my list of priorities.'

'Sixteen and three quarters,' hissed Gerald's scandalized voice in stereo from directly behind the back of my head.

Reverend Spool beamed in appreciation of my magnificent gesture, and said roguishly and somewhat confusingly, 'Yes, yes, no, no, well, well, we shall see. By the way, we are planning to tape-record the service as usual for the homebound. I trust you have no objection to that?' (vaguely) 'No problems with er ... copyright?'

Said, 'No, of course not.'

Thought, Oh, thank *you,* God! They're going to carefully preserve my humiliation and pass it round the universe.

Nearly died of nerves as I sat on one of the front pews next to Gerald waiting for the service to start. All the small children had been shepherded into the front five or six rows on the other side by lady helpers, and already one or two of them were pointing me, a stranger, out to each other, and producing giggling mini-explosions as though there was something excruciatingly funny about the way I looked. Those little monsters were never going to listen attentively to anything I said to them, for heaven's sake!

Wondered again – how *could* I have been so stupid?

A little distracted, thank goodness, after things got started, by Reverend Spool's notices.

Later, Gerald said that they were even more vicarishly vicarish than the vicarishness he had witnessed from any number of very vicarish vicars in the past. He clearly thought this comment of *his* extremely funny, but when I riposted with an observation that he must be very fond of Vicarish Allsorts, he looked at me in a very puzzled way, as if I'd said something completely meaningless.

Spool's staggeringly convoluted notices, transcribed this afternoon by Gerald from the tape of the service, were as follows:

'Good morning. A few brief notices before our service commences.

'In the forthcoming week Tuesday will be the fourth Tuesday in a month that has five Tuesdays, so, as is our normal practice, we shall be bringing the Wednesday meeting back to Monday, and holding the Tuesday meeting on Friday. Please study these details carefully, as we wish to avoid the most unsatisfactory situation that occurred on the last occasion that Tuesday was the fourth Tuesday in a month of five Tuesdays, when a number of folk attended all four meetings in the hope that they might hit upon the right one by chance.

'I have been asked to remind everybody that the key to the side-chapel is on a hook in the junction box just outside the vestry door. The key to the junction box is kept in the tall cupboard at the back of the church, and the key to the tall cupboard can be found in the robing chest which is situated just outside the vestry door immediately beneath the junction box. The key to the robing chest is held by Mr Frobisher, who has kindly agreed to make it available for collection on the first and third Mondays and the second and fourth Tuesdays of each month. On those months which actually commence on a Monday the key will be available on the first Wednesday, the second Friday, the third Thursday and the fourth Wednesday of that month.

'The side-chapel has been rather underused of late, and we hope that more folk will take advantage of this facility.

'May I ask that, when the time comes for communion, those occupying the left-hand side of the rearmost block of pews should make their way up the north aisle, through the door into the passage between the church and the hall, turn right just past the disabled toilet, proceed round behind the altar and approach the rail through the north door of the Lady Chapel.

'It really is impossible, incidentally, to emphasize too strongly the need to remember that right turn immediately after passing the disabled toilet. The week before last Mr Tooley, whose sight is poor, failed to turn to the right, spent a lengthy and distressing time in the church boiler-room, and finally arrived at the altar rail just after the commencement of the opening hymn in the following service.

'Similarly, last week, Mrs Cardew-Fitt, who is really quite frail and elderly, and just a little confused, walked straight on out of the east door, and along the High Street, eventually lining up for communion in the public bar of the Blue Cockatoo. Both incidents very upsetting for all concerned, and quite unnecessary if the two people involved had borne these very clear instructions in mind.

'Procedure for those in the right-hand side of that rearmost block of pews is, if anything, even simpler. They should go out of the west door, circle around the building in an anti-clockwise direction, re-enter through the south door of the Lady Chapel, and, with due sensitivity to those of the left-hand side of the rearmost block of pews who might be passing through at that moment, approach via the north door of the chapel, bearing in mind as they do so, that folk from the main body of the church will be approaching and departing at the same time.

'It is, may I say, a matter for sad regret that some flippant person has seen fit to scrawl the words "COMMUNION CONGA – THIS WAY" on the passage wall. Communion is a solemn matter, and these measures are designed to ease the involvement of all in that solemnity.

'I am happy to announce that the new arrangements for after-church coffee are working extremely well. Each Sunday we are adding to the number of folk who want coffee and actually manage to get some.

'Finally, I am told that some people have expressed concern regarding the complicated nature of our arrangements here at St Dermot's. Well, you know, friends, if you don't come and tell me, your vicar, the things that are troubling you, how on earth am I ever going to find out? Eh? Come and talk it over. I am, as always, regularly available on the fifth, seventh and twelfth odd-numbered days in each month, other than those which fall on a weekend, except where that weekend is the penultimate weekend in the month, when such exceptions do not apply. Whatever the problem, I'm sure we can work it out – in time.

'Good – and now may I say, on behalf of all of us, and especially the little ones, how pleased we are to welcome Mr Adrian Plass, who will be doing our children's talk this morning. Mr Plass has written some gloriously funny books and is well known as a very fine speaker, so we all look forward with immense pleasure to hearing what he has to say to us.

Thank you.'

Nearly paralysed with nerves by the time I stood up to talk to the children. Felt as if I was trying to swallow a large apple whole, smile and speak simultaneously. Decided the only hope of keeping their attention was to make an impact right at the beginning.

I said, 'Right, who'd like to hear a *really* scary story?'

So far, so good. All the children and a selection of indulgently smiling, roguishly uninhibited, crinkly-eyed adults put their hands up.

'The only thing is – I'm not sure if I ought to tell you this story, because it's very, very, *very* frightening. In fact it's *so* frightening that I might make myself scream with fear just by telling it to you. In fact, it's probably the most terrifying story *anyone, anywhere* has *ever* heard in the whole history of telling stories.'

Certainly seemed to have succeeded in making an impact on everybody. Noticed that the indulgent smiles on the faces of most of the crinkly-eyed adults had faded. A small, round-faced, rosy-cheeked, pigtailed girl of about three glanced worriedly over her shoulder to check Mummy and Daddy were still in the church.

I said, in low, menacing tones, 'Ready to be sick with fear, then?'

Might have overdone it a bit. The children were a solid block of tension and dread, holding on to each other for safety and staring at me, wide-eyed with apprehension. Certainly paying attention.

Ruined the whole effect right at the beginning with a stupid, unintentional spoonerism.

I said, 'Once upon a time, there was a crappy little gab called Hordon ...'

Short, shocked, uncomprehending silence. An elderly lady at the back of the church cupped her hand behind her ear and said, 'Once upon a time there was a *what,* did he say ... ?'

The small pigtailed girl turned round and said in a loud, clear voice, 'He said there was a crappy little gab called Hordon, but I don't know what crappy means, and I don't know what a gab is, and I've never heard of anyone called "Hordon". What is a crappy little gab called Hordon? What does *crappy* mean? Is it –'

Panicked and interrupted hurriedly. 'I didn't say the story was about a crappy little gab called Hordon.' Expressions of outraged disbelief appeared on the faces of the children. 'Or rather – sorry, sorry – I did say that, but it was a mistake. What I meant to say was that once upon a time there was a happy little crab called Gordon. And one day Gordon's big brothers and sisters forgot what their mummy and daddy had told them about looking after Gordon, and while they were doing something else he wandered off into a different rockpool and was very frightened because a seagull nearly ate him up and his mummy rescued him just in time.'

Short silence.

The little girl said, 'What happened next?'

'Er, well, that's it – that's the end.'

Filled with despair as I realized that I'd left out all the funny crab voices and the conversation between the brothers and sisters and the frightening bit leading up to Gordon's mummy finding him. I'd managed to finish the story in thirty seconds flat.

'That's not what I'd call a very, very *scary* story,' said the pig-tailed girl. 'That's what I'd call a very, very *short* story.'

Tried to carry brightly on.

'Right, now who'd like to suggest what the story teaches us?'

Lots of arms went up. Pointed at a thin little girl with huge glasses.

She said, 'The seaside is a very bad, nasty, dangerous place for small children?'

Two toddlers opened their eyes very wide at this suggestion and, to my horror, seemed to be on the verge of tears.

'No,' I said hurriedly, 'of course it doesn't mean that. The seaside is a *lovely* place for children. Of course it is.'

The two toddlers cheered up immediately. The thin little girl's face crumpled.

'But er ... it was a very good suggestion – very good indeed. Well done!' Could hear my own voice rising to a hysterical pitch. 'Come on, somebody else – what does the story show us?'

A little lad with wide staring eyes and hair standing up on end, who looked as if a powerful electric current was being passed through his body, called out, 'Does it show that we must never trust our brothers and sisters, because they just don't care when we get eaten at the seaside?'

Felt as if I was going mad. I know I'd started it, but the whole thing was turning into something out of Edgar Allan Poe. Children's talks aren't supposed to leave the congregation emotionally scarred for life.

'Of course our brothers and sisters care when we get eaten at the seaside. I mean' – hastily – 'we're not going to be eaten at the seaside – or anywhere else for that matter, but if we were – *if* we were, then our brothers and sisters would certainly care, of *course* they would. Look, doesn't anyone think,' I pleaded desperately, 'that the story might show how important it is for us to look after each other? Do you think that's what it shows?'

At this, a pretty little dark-haired thing pushed her hand into the air as far as it would go, waving wildly, rocking her whole body and clenching her teeth with the sheer eagerness of her desire to reply. I nodded encouragingly.

'Do you think that's what it shows?'

She said, 'No.'

Could feel my whole being moving rapidly into Basil Fawlty mode.

'All right – all right! Everybody put their hands down and I'll go over it again, okay? No, I said put your hands *down,* didn't I? You all had your chance to say what the story meant just now, and no one's got it right. Now it's my turn, unless of course someone wants to object.'

Glared challengingly at the children. They huddled fearfully together for mutual protection and said nothing.

'Now! There's a crab called Gordon. Right?'

Anxious nods.

'He's happy. *Right?*'

More nods.

'His brothers and sisters are supposed to be looking after him. Right? Anybody find that difficult to understand?'

Solemn head shakes.

'But they forget to look after him and he nearly gets eaten by a seagull. *Right?*'

Slightly more confident nods.

'But Gordon's mother rescues him. *Right?*'

Smiles and nods.

'Good! Excellent! So – what does the story teach us?'

Uneasy pause. Children all looked at each other. At last, a slightly odd, serious-looking, short-haired boy of about ten, dressed in a dark suit and tie, raised his hand.

'Yes?'

'It shows that Satan will sometimes appear to us as a seagull.'

Depressed silence.

Gave up, and said, 'Amen.'

Afterwards, Reverend Spool reacted as if I'd converted the whole of Great Britain.

'*Wonderful!*' he enthused, clasping my hand again, 'I'm sure our children were greatly challenged by your message. So much more likely that a lesson will lodge in tiny minds when it comes wrapped up in a well-told story.'

Frowns of annoyance directed at me from some of the parents who were trying to soothe their disturbed small children suggested that, given half a chance, they'd like to have lodged something in my tiny mind – a hatchet, for instance. Detached myself as soon as possible from the vicar, who said, just as we were going through the door, 'By the way, I have instructed Mr Frobisher that he is to ambush you – yes, positively to *ambush* you – before you leave the church premises. He will be thrilled to defray your expenses. Thank you so much for inspiring us. You must come and speak to the kiddies again soon ...'

Asked Gerald what he'd thought of my talk as we passed through the church porch.

He said, 'May I phrase my answer in the form of a cryptic crossword clue?'

Sighed. 'If you must.'

'Well, I think it would be something like this.'

Handed me another of his infernal backs-of-envelope-jottings.
I read it. It said:

RUBBISH FROM CANADA AND FAST MOVING RHYTHMIC
VERSE PERFORMED TO MUSICAL BACKING (4 LETTERS)

Gerald said, 'And the solution is – '

I said, 'I've solved it, thank you very much, and I agree.'

In the churchyard we were accosted by Mr Frobisher. He
turned out to be an immensely fat young man with a very small
purse, a common phenomenon among treasurers, perhaps, Gerald surmised rather obscurely later. Reverend Spool's assurance
that Mr Frobisher would be thrilled to defray our expenses
erred on the side of optimism. On the contrary, Mr Frobisher
seemed to regard us with deep suspicion, and, judging from his
general manner, was actually very reluctant indeed to defray
our expenses.

Having taken out a small notebook and pencil as well as the
small purse, he said in a high-pitched, officious voice, 'May I
enquire as to the fee?'

I went through my modest, head-shaking, no-need-to-bother
routine, but he didn't even try to argue. He just moved on to the
next question.

'May I enquire as to the means of transport?'

Gerald twisted his head round until he was looking at the page
on which Mr Frobisher was about to write, and said in friendly,
helpful, I'll-say-it-and-you-write-it-down tones, 'Er, we came by
helicopter. That's h, e, l, i – '

'We came by car!' I interrupted hurriedly, as Mr Frobisher
started to inflate to an even greater size. 'And there's no need to
pay us anything for that. The trip is no more than seven-eighths
of a mile – it's not worth bothering with, really it's not.'

'The Reverend has instructed me that I am to defray your travelling expenses,' squeaked Mr Frobisher, 'and we pay thirty pence
for every mile travelled. In this case the total mileage comes to
twice seven-eighths of a mile which is fourteen-eighths of a mile
which is one mile plus six-eighths of a mile which is –'

Forced to stop because he couldn't work out the sum in his head, Mr Frobisher produced from his pocket a calculator as minuscule as the rest of his equipment, stuck his tongue out of the side of his mouth and prodded buttons for a moment.

'That comes,' he said at last, 'to fifty-two and a half pence. I feel sure Reverend Spool would wish me to round that up to fifty-three pence.'

Solemnly, he counted the coins into my hand before producing a Lilliputian receipt book, which I duly and solemnly signed.

'Well,' said Gerald, as we climbed into the car, 'that was a nice little earner, wasn't it? Fifty-three pence! Wow!'

'There's one consolation,' I replied.

'Which is?'

'That's just a little more than my talk was actually worth . . .'

## Monday 14 March

Felt embarrassed this morning just thinking about yesterday's fiasco. Not helped by Gerald pointing out that, as I owe him a bottle of claret, I'm actually about four pounds out of pocket. All

I could see in the bathroom mirror was a crappy little gab called Adrian. At breakfast Anne was quite sympathetic (now that I've done it!), but she said it's all part of learning what my limitations are, and then saying 'No' to things that I've got no talent for.

I said, 'But we're not supposed to limit God, are we?'

Gerald chipped in and said, 'No, but if Moses had decided to bake a chocolate cake gigantic enough to feed several hundred thousand Israelites just at the point when he was supposed to be getting on with parting the Red Sea, I don't think there would have been any culinary miracles available, do you? God would have got cross and made it sink in the middle.'

He paused, then said reflectively, 'I feel really sorry for old Moses, you know. Fancy going all that way and then not being allowed to enter the Promised Land. Can't you just picture him standing up on Mount Nebo, a hundred and twenty years old, eyesight as good as ever, gazing out at Naphtali, and Manasseh, and Judah stretching all the way to the Mediterranean, and the Negeb and the Jordan Valley and Jericho and Zoar, and realizing he'd never get there? And then, like a sort of Old Testament Frank Sinatra, knowing it was his last appearance, he'd have turned to the hordes of Israelites down on the plain and sung the old song just one more time.'

'Old song? What old song?'

'I did it Ya-a-a-hweh!' warbled Gerald.

## Tuesday 15 March

Happened to mention to Gerald this morning that an awful lot of the Christians I meet don't seem to feel they've ever really met God and been properly forgiven by him. You'd think, I said, that Jesus had never told the story of the Prodigal Son. When I got back tonight from a Glander-filled day, he showed me another of these Scripture rewrites of his. Said our chat in the morning had inspired him. Felt quite flattered really.

Oddest feeling is creeping up on me that Gerald is the adult around here, and I'm a sort of earnest adolescent. Quite nice in a way – I think.

At last he cometh to his senses and saith, 'All my father's hired workers have more than they can eat, and here am I about to starve! I will arise and go to my father and say, "Father, I have sinned against heaven and before thee. I am no longer worthy to be called thy son; make me as one of thy hired servants."'

So he arose and came to his father.

But when he was still a long way off his father seeth him and runneth to him and falleth on his neck and pulleth his hair and smacketh his backside and clumpeth him on the ear and saith, 'Where the devil do you think you've been, Scumbag?'

And the prodigal replieth, 'Father, I have sinned against heaven and before thee. I am no longer worthy to be called thy son; make me as one of thine hired servants.'

The father saith, 'Too right I'll make thee as one of my hired servants, Master Dirty-stop-out-inheritance-spending-stinker-pinker-prodigal! I suppose thou believest that thou canst waltz back in here without so much as an by thine leave, and conneth me with thine dramatic little speech? Thinkest thou that this is "Little House on the Prairie"? Or mayhap thou reckoneth that I was born yestere'en? Oh, no. Third assistant bog-cleaner, unpaid, for thee, mine odorous ex-relative.'

Then the prodigal saith dismally unto him, 'Oh, right, right – fair enough. So, er, just to get it straight, there existeth no question of lots of nice presents and instant forgiveness and an large celebratory meal involving the fatted calf, or anything of that nature?'

'In thy dreams, son!' replieth the father. 'The only gift thou art likely to see is the personalized lavatory-brush with which thou shalt shortly be presented.'

And the father taketh the prodigal by that ear which previously he clumpeth, and hauleth him back to the farm.

And lo, the fatted calf beholdeth them approach from an long way off, and, summing up the situation perfectly, throweth an big party. And the fatted calf's family and guests rejoiceth and doeth an bit of discow-dancing, and mooeth sarcastically over the fence at the prodigal as he passeth by in his tribulation.

And behold, as nightfall approacheth, the prodigal's elder brother heareth distant sounds as of an bog-brush being applied, and strolleth out to the edge of the cess-pit after supper holding an large brandy, and he stretcheth luxuriously and picketh his teeth and lighteth an enormous cigar and looketh down and saith, 'Evenin', Rambo. I see thou hast returned, then? Likest thou thine rapid progress from affluent to effluent?'

And the prodigal looketh up and saith, 'Verily, thou rebukest me justly with thine clever barb. When I had great wealth I shared it not with thee, but now I freely offer thee an good share of what is mine.'

And he flicketh at the elder brother with his brush, so that an weighty portion of something exceeding unpleasant ploppeth into his brother's brandy glass, and his brother retireth, threatening to tell on him.

And the prodigal findeth his father and saith unto him, 'Behold, all these years during which I was in an far country, mine smug, pie-faced, hypocritical, dipstick of an brother must have caused thee to gnash thine teeth on an daily basis, so how come he getteth all the perks like brandy, cigars and suchlike, while I remaineth up to mine elbows in other people's poo?'

But his father replieth, 'Thine brother is boring but biddable. Get on with thine work, thou less than Baldrick, and think thyself lucky.'

The father departeth and the prodigal saith to himself, 'Blow this for an game of centurions. I wisheth I hadn't come home now. Behold I am just as hungry, twice as guilty and four times as smelly. Verily, if, by an miracle, any time off ever presenteth itself, there existeth in my mind no doubt about how I shall seek to occupieth it. Definitely – it's an day-trip to the pigs for me . . .'

## Wednesday 16 March

Spent quite a long time today trying to work out whether the sort of thing Gerald wrote yesterday means that he's getting closer to God or further away. At teatime, when he wasn't around, I said to Anne, 'I think Peter O'Sullevan's going to get his knickers in a real twist over Gerald's Future.'

She said, 'Past experience tells me, darling, that what you've just said almost certainly means something to you, even though it appears to be complete nonsense to me. Unravel your thought processes gently and I might even end up agreeing with you.'

She did.

## Thursday 17 March

Thynn round today. Cornered him in the sitting-room.

I said casually, 'Oh, by the way, Leonard, I've worked out why the thing about Percy Brain's roof made you all laugh so much.'

'Oh, you have, have you?' said Leonard. 'Well, what was it, then?'

Said I'd hit him if he didn't tell me, but Anne and Gerald burst in and rescued him. The three of them put me under the cushions on the settee, then sat on me and said my attempt to trick the information out of Thynn was a futile gesture. Not something St Paul ever had to put up with. He never denied his faith when he was being shipwrecked, beaten, starved or imprisoned, but if he'd had to endure being put under sofa cushions and sat on by his immediate family and friends who wouldn't tell him what their stupid joke meant, it might have been a different story.

He and I could swop a few yarns . . .

## Friday 18 March

Going out for an Indian meal later this evening with Anne, Leonard, Gerald, Edwin and Richard (Doreen wouldn't come, but I don't know why) as a sort of get-together before our big trip to Australia next week.

I enjoy Indian food very much – I mean *very* much, but the business of ordering it drives me completely mad. I start getting

tense long before we leave home. Can't bear the prospect of everyone fussing and faffing around with the menus, choosing something at last, then changing their minds, then changing their
minds back again, then forgetting what they've decided as soon
as the waiter comes. And as for the business of paying – oh, the
whole thing really does drive me round the bend.

Decided to prevent all the hassle this time.

Waited until about five o'clock when Anne and Gerald went
off to the supermarket, then rang Edwin, and asked him to choose
within the next half hour what he was going to have and tell me
what he'd decided when I rang him back. Sounded a little surprised but said he'd do his best.

Then I rang Leonard. Speaking to Thynn by phone is like using
a megaphone to communicate with another planet – a complete
waste of time. The conversation went as follows:

ME: Hello, Leonard, is that you?

THYNN: Yes, it's me.

ME: I want to talk about tonight.

THYNN: All right, then.

ME: You haven't forgotten, have you?

THYNN: Oh, good.

ME: Well, it's not good if you have forgotten – so have you?

THYNN: I don't know.

ME: You don't know what?

THYNN: I don't know if I've forgotten, because I can't remember what it is I'm supposed to have not forgotten.

ME: You haven't forgotten what's happening tonight.

THYNN: What is happening tonight?

ME: Leonard, you *know* what's happening tonight.

THYNN: I don't know what's happening. I've forgotten.

ME: We're going out for an Indian.

THYNN: I'm sorry, George, I can't – I'm already going out for an
Indian with Adrian and Anne and the others.

ME: This is Adrian speaking, you blithering idiot!

THYNN: Oh, sorry, I thought you were George, but – hold on a minute – if you're Adrian, you *know* what we're doing tonight.

ME: Well, of course I know that I know, don't I! I was just checking that – oh, never mind. Listen, Leonard, I want you to tell me what you'd like to eat tonight.

THYNN: Well, personally, I'd be quite happy with an Indian meal.

ME: (PAUSING TO GRIND THE TIP OF A PENCIL INTO THE BRICK-WORK UNDER THE WINDOW-SILL) Leonard, tell me which main dish you would like to eat at the Indian restaurant tonight or I shall come round there and puree you in your own blender.

THYNN: (PANICKING A LITTLE) Sweet and sour pork would be fine.

ME: That's Chinese.

THYNN: No it's not, it's English. I said –

ME: Sweet and sour pork is a Chinese dish. Which Indian dish would you like?

THYNN: (A WILD GUESS) Tandoori, then?

ME: Tandoori is a generic term.

THYNN: That's fine – I like it generic. Can I have pilau rice with it, and lots of poppadoms to start?

ME: (CURIOUSLY NUMBED) Tandoori is a style of cooking. I'll put you down for a chicken tikka, shall I, Leonard?

THYNN: Oh, yes, fine, if you think I'd like that better than a – a geriatric tern, was it? I don't think I fancy that much anyway, now I think about it. Sounds vile, but I suppose if you're very poor in India and you live by the sea, you have to –

ME: (WEAKLY INTERRUPTING) I'll see you at eight o'clock tonight at the restaurant, Leonard. You know which one we're going to, don't you?

THYNN: Yes, the one next to the cinema.

ME: That's right, it's called All the Raj. See you later.

THYNN: See you later.

After recovering from my dialogue with Thynn I rang Richard at work and asked him what he fancied. After a brief but utterly ludicrous discussion on the dangers of accidentally ingesting occult spices, he settled on a prawn biryani with a stuffed paratha. Wrote it down carefully.

Rang Edwin back and asked if he'd chosen his food. Hallelujah! He had. He went for a tandoori mixed grill with a main-course vegetable curry and nan bread.

Began to feel quite optimistic about the coming evening, although I knew I still had the toughest nuts to crack. Somehow I had to find out what Anne and Gerald were likely to order without them realizing what I was doing. Devised a cunning plan.

When they came back with the shopping and I was helping to carry the bags through to the kitchen, I said casually, 'I suppose you two wouldn't rather give the Indian a miss this evening? We could go to a pub or something instead.'

Went on stowing stuff away in the larder and fridge, conscious that Gerald and Anne were standing in flabbergasted silence behind me. Turned round and noticed them.

'What?'

'Dad,' said Gerald at last, 'I can't believe you're saying this. You salivate like a starving mongrel at the very mention of Indian food.'

'Thank you for that delicate observation, Gerald,' I replied, 'and you're quite right usually, of course. It's just that – well, I've tried most things on the menu and I'm getting a bit bored. Time for a change, perhaps.'

Anne shook her head disbelievingly and said, 'Darling, you have *not* tried most things on the menu. On the contrary, you choose precisely the same things every single time we go.'

'Mum's right, Dad,' contributed Gerald, 'you're more regular than a Prussian on a diet of prunes.'

'Well, what do you suggest I have then? What are you both going to eat?'

'I know what I'm going to have,' said Anne. 'I don't want any old pub dinner. I want chicken korma and that lovely lentil dish and lots of special rice, and I'm going to have it, so there!'

'Come on, Dad,' coaxed Gerald, 'you know you want to go really. Have the same as me. I'm going for lamb curry and those onion things that look like balls of shoelaces tied together, and about a million poppadoms with that heavenly mango chutney.'

Tried not to let them see my mouth watering.

'Oh, all right,' I conceded, 'we'll go to the Indian. After all, Edwin and Richard and Leonard are probably looking forward to it. Can't let them down.'

Hurried upstairs to jot down Anne and Gerald's choices. Felt quietly triumphant. Nice to leave my wife and son feeling a trifle bewildered for a change. I'll write about the meal when I get back.

*11:30 p.m.*

Some are born ignominious, some achieve ignominy, some have ignominy thrust upon them. I must be one of the very few people in the history of the world who qualify on all three counts.

If only I'd bothered to check that the sheet of paper I picked up before we left for the restaurant was the one with the list of Indian dishes on it. The one I actually grabbed came from the same jotting pad, the one beside our bed, and was also a list, written with the same pen. Because, as usual, we were in a tearing hurry, I snatched it up quickly and just assumed I'd got the right one. Even then it might not have been so bad if I'd taken the trouble to glance at the stupid thing in All the Raj before handing it to the waiter with – well, I suppose it might have appeared a rather lordly air. I'd so enjoyed producing it with a flourish and announcing that menus would not be necessary because I had a complete list of everyone's requirements. I wasn't even too put out by Anne's glare of disapproval. I felt good, a bit like Hercule Poirot at the end of a book, blinding the assembled company with his brilliance.

The difference between the great detective and me being, of course, that he was a private dick, whereas I was about to perform in public.

The smartly dressed waiter took my sheet of paper and studied it attentively for a moment or two. A puzzled expression appeared on his polite features.

He said, 'Please excuse me, sir, but this food order begins itself with "Widgeon's bottom", and finishes itself with "Moving parts in oil". Neither of these are common Indian dishes.'

I snatched the piece of paper from his hand.

Anne said, 'You've brought your list of weekend-jobs-to-avoid-at-all-costs by mistake, haven't you? Serves you right!'

Everyone in stitches. Gerald loved it, of course. Wanted to know what 'Widgeon's bottom' could possibly mean. Explained with what rags of dignity remained to me, that Stephanie Widgeon had asked me if I would clear the end of her garden so that she could grow vegetables. Declined to explain 'Moving parts in oil' on the grounds that there had already been enough hilarity at my expense.

Thynn nearly got us thrown out at this point. He said that it didn't matter me bringing the wrong list because we could probably all remember what we'd ordered.

'Take me, for instance,' he said, turning to speak to the waiter. 'I'm pretty sure I can remember what I was having.'

The patient waiter poised his pen above his order pad respectfully.

'Yes,' said Thynn, assuming a ridiculously unconvincing man of the world air. 'Adrian tells me that one of your specialities is elderly seagull cooked in the tandoori style.'

A sort of microcosmic Indian Mutiny was only avoided by giving the impression to the deeply affronted waiter and two of his colleagues who were summoned to witness this vile slander against the establishment, that Leonard was a sadly deranged but harmless person who was in the habit of making wild, meaningless statements (more or less true, come to think of it) and that we were present in the role of keepers or minders.

Felt a bit guilty about this. Tried to explain to Leonard, but he was so inextricably confused that I had to abandon the attempt to take him on a mental journey from 'generic term' to 'elderly seagull', and simply said it had all been my fault, which, of course, as Anne unhesitatingly pointed out, it had.

Felt a bit depressed after that, not least because we still had to go through the whole nerve-jangling business of ordering, but I didn't dare utter a word of complaint.

Edwin must have realized that I was feeling a bit low. Once we had our food in front of us, he took a postcard from his inside pocket and held it up. On one side there was a picture of semi-naked African dancers.

'Look at this,' said Edwin, 'it arrived from Victoria Flushpool in Africa this morning. I'll read you what she says:

> 'Dear Edwin and all at church,
> Work going very well here.
> Great blessings. Impertinent
> mosquitoes. Watched this tribal
> dancing on Tuesday. Enthusiasm
> and modesty disproportionately
> related. Stenneth studying
> Titus as before. Africa needs
> a good clean. Have begun.
>     Love, Victoria.'

Anne, Leonard and I burst into laughter on hearing the contents of the postcard. Even Richard emitted a restrained, hissing little chuckle. Gerald looked blank.

He said, 'What are you all laughing at? I mean – it's quite funny, but nothing to get hysterical about – is it?'

Edwin said, 'Oh, it's just the bit about Stenneth and Titus. If you ever wanted cast-iron evidence that Victoria has genuinely changed for the better, it's the fact that she can mention something like that in a postcard for the whole church to see. Wonderful, really.'

Gerald still looked blank. 'I don't know what you're talking about, Edwin. What about Stenneth and Titus?'

Suddenly realized that Gerald had not been at church on the memorable occasion to which Edwin was referring. In fact, he had been away from home altogether on some kind of hiking holiday with William Farmer. Wondered why I'd never told him, but I knew the answer even as I asked myself the question. He would have made *such* a meal of it.

I said, 'Gerald never heard what happened that day, Edwin. You tell him.'

'All right,' agreed Edwin, 'as long as Anne doesn't mind. It's a bit er . . .'

Anne laughed and said, 'Edwin, the expression on Victoria's face that morning is one of the memories I use to cheer myself up with when life is at its darkest. I'm glad we didn't tell you about it at the time, though, Gerald.'

'All right, then,' said Edwin, 'I'm sure Victoria wouldn't object to me talking about it now. I'll tell you what happened, but don't blame me if I collapse before I get to the end.'

Before starting he gazed into the distance for a moment with an almost beatific smile on his face.

'It was several years ago on a Sunday towards the end of August, and a lot of folk were still away on their holidays, so there weren't all that many people there. Stenneth was supposed to be doing a sort of little Bible-study during the service, not the actual message, because – well, frankly, at that time I wasn't very keen on the idea of exposing the church to what you might call the Flush-pool way of thinking. But Victoria had been going on and on at me all year about letting Stenneth get involved in "the ministry of the word". Not, she insisted, that the impetus came from her, because that would not have been Scriptural. No, Stenneth was the head of the woman, and woe betide him if he dared to argue the point. So, in the end, I gave in, and offered Stenneth this particular Sunday just because I knew it wouldn't be all that well attended. To be quite honest, poor old Stenneth didn't want to do it anyway, but he was a man under orders, and, as he put it, rather dolefully, "Most of the choices I'm allowed to make in life are between one thing that I don't want, and another thing that I want even less."

'Now, the other thing you need to know, Gerald, is that the Flushpools themselves had come back from holiday on the Friday just gone, and –'

'They didn't used to call them holidays, though, did they?' interrupted Gerald. 'Didn't they call them "periods of recreational outreach"?'

'That's right,' agreed Edwin, chuckling, 'recreational outreach, that was it. Well, this particular period of recreational outreach was a prize that Victoria and Stenneth had won in some kind of competition – can't have been a raffle, because raffles were about on a par with mass murder on the sin scale – anyway, they won it, and, after a lot of iffing and butting and persuading on my part, they decided to go. It was a week at one of those sunny Mediterranean resorts, and it was only after they'd gone that I suddenly realized the beaches near their hotel were pretty well bound to be full of topless bathers. I had this picture in my mind of Stenneth, still formally dressed in suit and tie, sitting on a deckchair with his gaze rigidly fixed on the far horizon, with Victoria in very close attendance, grimly policing the movement of his eyeballs.'

We all sat in fascinated silence for a moment, picturing the scene as Edwin had described it.

'Well,' continued Edwin, 'somehow, not via me, I can assure you, word got around that the Flushpools had gone off to a nudey-beach in the South of France, and by the time they came back there were a number of jokes on the subject in currency, and I had to actually ask some people to cool it a bit, because I didn't want Victoria and Stenneth to get upset.

'So, Sunday morning comes along, and old Stenneth had decided he was going to say a bit about the New Testament book that he'd been reading and thinking about in his devotional time during the holiday. Give him due credit – on the Saturday he'd contacted five small children of parents who'd definitely be there that weekend – it was Family Service, you understand – and asked them to help him introduce his subject. Then, on the Sunday morning, just before the service began, he gave each child a large

110

square made of card with a letter on it to hold up when he began his talk . . .'

A sudden convulsion of laughter choked Edwin for a moment. He pulled himself together and continued.

'Sorry about that. The first bit of the service went all right, and then it was time for Stenneth to do his stuff. Victoria was sitting right up on the front row, ready to fuel her husband with the power of visible expectation, as it were, and Stenneth was shuffling pieces of paper nervously, trying to find the courage to actually open his mouth and say something. Then he got going at last.

'He said, "May I ask the children at the back to join me up here, so that everyone can see what we shall be talking about."

'So this little troop of children marched solemnly up to the front and positioned themselves in a neat line to the side of and just behind Stenneth, holding their cards down ready for when they were told to lift them up.

'"Right, children," said Stenneth brightly, ignoring the fact that the children were looking mildly perturbed about something, "show everybody what I've been studying all this last week on holiday."

'When the children lifted their cards they should, of course, have spelled out the word "TITUS". They didn't. Unfortunately for Stenneth, "U" had nipped into the lavatory just before being called up, and the ensuing gap was –' he nearly choked again ' – a rather significant one.'

I have never seen Gerald laugh as much as he did when Edwin came to this point in his story. He ended up quite red in the face, and had to be patted on the back and told to sip water. When he'd recovered, he asked Edwin how the rest of the congregation had reacted.

'Well, all I can say is that human beings are capable of quite incredible restraint on certain occasions. I don't think anyone actually laughed out loud at that point, but when "U" suddenly came rushing from the toilet to take up his position between "T" and "S" one of the teenagers at the back just seemed to burst. She put her head down in her lap, and started to literally sob with laughter. Stenneth, who still had no idea what was going on, asked for someone to take her off into another room for ministry. How the rest of us kept straight faces I shall never know. There was a tremendous feeling of togetherness in church that day – the fellowship of suffering and all that, I suppose. But, oh, my, what a moment!' He held up the postcard again. 'And that's why this means so much.'

'Goodness, yes,' said Anne, 'at the time Victoria was in a state of utter dumbfoundedness. She looked like someone who wants to blame the council for a mountain falling on her head but knows in her heart that it was an act of God.'

'Perhaps it was,' smiled Edwin.

When we got home tonight Gerald said to me, 'There's one other question that I'd have asked about the Titus episode.'

'Yes,' I said, 'what's that?'

'Which inspired member of the congregation bribed "U" to disappear with such perfect timing?'

## Saturday 19 March

Frantic preparation for Australia. We're allowed one large suitcase and one small bag each. I hate packing. It's like a grenade going off in a jumble sale. Left it to Anne.

Thynn, very proud of himself, brought his case round this evening and asked Anne to check it. She found it was full of thick pullovers and scarves and fishermen's socks and a very large overcoat. Anne gently pointed out that Australians would be in the middle of their summer, so we'd be wearing shorts and tee-shirts most of the time. Thynn laughed as though she'd made a really funny joke. Spent the next half hour helping Leonard to catch up with Galileo. Only about four hundred years late.

Anne went home with Leonard to sort him out, then brought him back to stay tonight and tomorrow night.

We really are going!

How come the only person in Great Britain who still qualifies for the Flat Earth Society understands a joke about futile gestures, and I don't?

## Sunday 20 March

Edwin called Anne and me and Gerald and Leonard up to the front in church this morning and said a blessing over us. Felt very weepy and uncertain suddenly. Suppose Britain sinks while we're away?

Went for a walk after lunch. Wonder why I've never noticed how attractive our home town is before? All those nice, safe, familiar buildings and trees and streets and people. Wish something would happen to stop us going.

The night's come now. Help me, Jesus, I'm frightened.

## Monday 21 March

Mornings are magic. Yesterday's fears all disappeared with the night.

Good luck card from Stephanie Widgeon through the door just before we left. Little note on the bottom urging us to bear in mind that the church is not the building but the people. Beginning to annoy me a bit now.

Drove to Heathrow in the afternoon feeling very excited. Plane took off at about ten-thirty in the evening.

We've been on this plane now for about six weeks. During the early part of the trip I walked up the gangway to the toilet three times, but couldn't work out how to get in. Did a lot of stretching and deep breathing outside the door each time to convince people that I'd just come for a little exercise. Finally managed to open one, then couldn't for the life of me discover how to get out. Spent half an hour in there (missed four meals) before Anne sent a stewardess to see if I was all right. Very embarrassing. Guided me carefully back to my seat from behind as if I were suffering from some severe mental deficiency.

Got back to find Leonard, still coiled and folded into his sardine-class seat-space, muttering to himself with his eyes closed. Tapped him on the shoulder and asked what he was doing.

He said, 'I'm doing what Jesus said we must do.'

'Which is?'

'Praying for the people I hate.'

I said, 'And who are they?'

'First-class passengers.'

Think I've mastered the toilets now.

Anne and Gerald have been asleep for three or four hours. Very tempted to wake them and tell them that I haven't. All there has ever been or ever will be is this plane droning dozily on through the night, pretending to be on its way to Australia.

## Tuesday 22 March

Can't work out whether Tuesday is now Monday, Wednesday or still Tuesday, but a different bit of Tuesday than it would have been if we were still in England. All I want in the world is a space big enough to be horizontal in.

## Wednesday 23 March

Landed at last. Everything in me said it was time to go to bed, but everything around me said it was time to get up. Came out of the airport terminal at Perth into heat that hit me on the head like a hammer. Met by our hosts who were kindness itself. Took us to their big shady house with a swimming pool and sunbeds and lots of cold drinks and cicadas chirruping, and were told to relax and take it easy for the rest of the day.

Jet lag is a very strange sensation. Your will takes a step forward, or reaches out for a drink, but then you have to wait a second or two for it to actually happen. Like being in a dream.

Thynn rather disconcerted to find that our hosts' two children, little girls of about five and six, came running out to the back when they came home from school, and stood staring at him in awe.

They said, 'Are you really Leonard Thynn?'

Leonard said, 'Well, yes, I am.'

They said, 'Do you want to borrow our cat?' then burst into giggles and ran back inside.

Naturally I didn't mind the fact that they didn't come and gaze at *me* in awe – much. I mean, why should they? After all, I only wrote the books, didn't I?

Should get a really good sleep tonight – looking forward to the play tomorrow. Hopefully, my shy yes-it's-me-but-I'm-no-different-from-anyone-else-look will be a bit more effective there than it was at the Reginald and Eileen Afternoon Tea Club.

## Thursday 24 March

Off to Bongalinga Creek this afternoon. Had to leave fairly early. Apparently, when Australians say somewhere is 'just down the road' they could mean anything from fifty to five hundred miles.

What a welcome we got at the theatre! Had a huge seafood meal with the whole cast and technical crew before the performance. These Ozzies really know how to look after you. Thought personally that Thynn was a bit flamboyant. He'd bought a big bush hat complete with corks and insisted on wearing it to the theatre. They seemed to think he was wonderful, though. Hung on his every word. Very nice to the rest of us, but there was no doubt about who the star was. They laughed at everything he said as though it was a marvellous witticism, including his request for exact directions to Ramsey Street, which was just as well, because he was dead serious.

Play went ever so well, and the audience gave us a round of applause at the end, as well as giving a standing ovation to the cast.

Compared notes afterwards when we got back to the house where we were staying.

I said, 'The person who played you was really good, Leonard. It's amazing that he'd never met you before – it was so like you.'

'I don't think so,' said Leonard rather indignantly, 'the Leonard Thynn in the play was a strange, loony sort of person who kept getting in everyone's way and didn't know what he was talking about half the time.'

I laughed and said that proved my point. Leonard got quite annoyed. Said that the person who played me in the play was even more like me than the person who'd played him was like him.

What nonsense!

'The character who had the same name as me,' I said, 'was a pedantic, stolid, po-faced, self-deluded type of individual who was incapable of seeing things happening right in front of his face. Amiable in a bovine sort of way, but basically thick. Now you're not seriously trying to tell me that I'm like that, are you?'

There was a short silence, then Anne said, 'Let's talk about something else, shall we?'

So like Anne to rescue Leonard from getting too embarrassed.

## Friday 25 March

Free time today. Seem to have woken up properly now. Did a little tour of the city – so beautiful. Thynn on and on about the heat. Had a point, though. Couldn't spend long in direct sunshine. Temperature was up near the thirty degree mark during most of the day, and beyond for some of the time.

Decided to visit one of Perth's fine art galleries this afternoon. Not at all Thynn's cup of tea, really, so I was amazed and rather pleased to spot him in the distance standing, quite motionless, in front of one of the exhibits, staring straight at it with an expression of ecstatic rapture on his face. Moved a little closer to find out which particular work of art was so enthralling him. Appeared from a distance to be some sort of abstract, a rectangular, box-like shape filled with rows of little square apertures. Didn't want to get too close in case I broke the spell for him.

Whispered to Gerald, 'Look at that! Leonard's really taken with that modern piece. What is it about that particular exhibit that happens to speak just to him? I wonder what it's called?'

Gerald peered at Leonard's abstract and said dryly, 'I don't think that particular piece has a name, but if it did I think it would be simply entitled "Air-conditioning".'

## Saturday 26 March

*11:30 p.m.*

Really good meeting tonight at a little town just outside Perth. Felt quite proud of my little team, who sold books and showed people to seats and generally helped out.

Had to reject one of Thynn's loony schemes before we got going. Keeps coming up with 'tricks' at the moment to help with the speaking. Wish he wouldn't.

I was on my own in the little room at the back just before we were due to start, when he came rushing in clutching a book in one hand and half a large onion in the other.

Held the onion in front of my face and said, 'Use this!'

Looked at him blankly. Can't help feeling sometimes that, on some far distant planet, way out in space, an alien being is wondering why Leonard has been away from home for so long.

'Use what?' I said.

'This onion!' he said with wild enthusiasm. 'I bought it today. Use it just before the bit where you always make your voice break.'

'I do not *make* my voice break, Leonard,' I said with dignity. 'If and when my voice breaks, it is with genuine emotion.'

'Well, use it just before the bit where you always make your voice break with genuine emotion,' he persisted.

*Hate* it when Thynn says things like that. So diminishing. Very tempted to insert the half onion into him. Resisted the temptation. You're supposed to pray and meditate before talking about God, not insert vegetables into people. Decided to explore the fog of his mind.

I said, 'Leonard, please tell me as quietly and clearly as you can how I could possibly think half an onion essential to the success of my talk this evening.'

'You rub it on your hymnbook before you go on,' he said, in the tone of voice you use when someone is being wilfully dense.

'Rub it on my hymnbook?'

'Rub it on your hymnbook, yes, and then, when you come to the bit where you always – where you always *genuinely* make your voice break, put the open book over your face as if you're really upset and sniff the page you rubbed the onion on. People like tears, don't they? They'll think you really mean what you say. Good for business.'

'Good for business?' Shook my head in disbelief. Couldn't think of anything else to say.

'I read about it in this book I brought with me from England,' continued Thynn. 'There are lots of good tips in here.'

Took the book from his hand. It was a faded paperback printed in the fifties entitled 'HOW TO BE A SUCCESSFUL EVANGELIST' by someone called Conroy Orville Nathanburger the Third. Opened it at random and read the following passage aloud:

' . . . as the close of the meeting approaches, close your eyes tightly to indicate that you are concentrating on the instructions of a mystical inner voice. In suitably hushed and solemn tones, request all present to bow their heads and close their eyes while God ministers to his people. After a short but – hopefully – significant pause, invite those who feel that God has touched them to raise a hand in grateful acknowledgement, whilst insisting quite sternly that all eyes should remain shut. It may be necessary at this point to, as it were, "massage" the response of your congregation. I myself find it most helpful, if no hands at all are raised, to murmur humbly, warmly and appreciatively, such phrases as, "Thank you, Sir. Thank you, Madam. Thank you, young person – your obedience will bring you great blessing." This mild and harmless deception is guaranteed to have an almost magically stimulating effect on reluctant congregations . . .'

Leonard said, 'Good stuff, eh?'

'No, Leonard,' I replied, 'it is not "good stuff". It is appalling, dreadful stuff. I don't want to deceive people – I want to tell them the truth.'

Anne and Gerald came in at that moment to say it was time for the meeting to start. Anne asked what we were doing.

I said, 'I'm just explaining to Leonard that anyone the Lord's calling to salvation will come to faith whether or not I deceive them with an onion.'

Gerald and Anne studied me for a moment before exchanging the kind of pitying, concerned look that has been part of my life since Gerald was about six. Occurred to me that I might not have communicated with total clarity. Was going to explain, but Gerald didn't give me a chance.

'You know, Dad, you're a sort of theological Captain Kirk, aren't you? Boldly going where no man has gone before. I don't suppose anyone else has yet had the courage or the – the originality, to seriously tackle the shamefully unacknowledged problem of onion deception in the modern church. How will you go about it? I suppose the evil will have to be exposed layer by layer.'

Was about to thank Gerald for his rather heavy-handed satire, and point out that there was a perfectly reasonable explanation for what I'd said, when I suddenly heard myself being introduced and had to go.

Explained to Anne later.

Really excellent evening after Thynn's nonsense. Lots of laughter and a few tears – even without the onion. Australian people don't seem to mind you taking the mickey out of them as long as you begin by taking the mickey out of yourself. Things seem pretty good now as I lie in bed next to Anne writing this. And we've got seven days off with a borrowed, air-conditioned car to have a holiday. Thank you, God!

Won't bother with any more diary entries until next Friday, which is the day before my next meeting (a big one, apparently) is scheduled.

## Friday 1 April

Wonderful holiday travelling from motel to motel, falling into the pool at each one as soon as we arrived. Eating out at the excellent Sizzlers restaurants that serve steak and pasta and as much ice cream as you can eat. Walking through warm sea water on the edge of the ocean in the late evening. Cuddling koalas in sanctuaries. Trying to entice possums down from the roof with apple cores at night. Wrestling with the mosquitoes that love to eat pink, ripe poms. Even the 'mozzies' didn't put us off. We love Australia.

Rather surprised halfway through the week, when Gerald, who'd been scribbling on a piece of paper for the last five minutes or so, suddenly said, 'I think it ought to be a tour of New Zealand next year, Dad.'

Asked him why.

He said, 'Well, I've been reading about a place in New Zealand called Rotarua, a big tourist draw, apparently.'

'And you'd like to go there?'

'Only if I can go with a girl called Rhoda, or meet someone called Rhoda when I get there.'

'What – *any* girl called Rhoda?'

'Well, just three qualifications. She has to be more impolite and more likely to blush than another girl called Rhoda, she has to be willing to join us in a largish rowing boat some distance from Rotarua, and she has to be responsible for drawing up a list of pairs for rowing duty so that we can get there by sea.'

Stared at him for a moment. I said, 'You want me to ask you why, don't you?'

'Well, I've wasted a good ten minutes working this out if you don't.'

Sighed. 'All right, then, go on – why?'

'Because afterwards I want to be able to say – "The redder ruder Rhoda wrote a rota to row to Rotarua."'

You have to understand that it had been *very* hot ...

## Saturday 2 April

Rather taken aback by the size of the meeting tonight. Must have been about a thousand people there. Felt quite nervous looking out at such a vast sea of faces while the worship session was going on. Shut my eyes and tried to concentrate on God, but got distracted by the thought of how much money I'd have made if each person had paid three pounds to come in and I'd been due to get sixty per cent of the profits after all expenses on both sides had been taken out. Something like three thousand pounds minus, say, three hundred for their expenses and a couple of hundred for mine would have left something in the region of –

'Excuse me, brother, I know how important and precious time with the Lord is when you're about to speak, but I just wanted to make a quick point if you don't mind.'

It was the organizer of the meeting, Gary Turnbull, who was sitting next to me. Felt rather ashamed. Tried to look like someone who's been dragged back from the seventh heaven, but is willing to sacrifice further spiritual ecstasy for the sake of another's earthly needs. Crinkled my eyes and whispered, 'It's okay, carry on.'

He said, 'Just to let you know that we've allowed half an hour at the end for your ministry.'

Stared blankly at him.

I said, 'Oh, have you? Er . . . what is that, then? When you say my ministry, you mean er . . . ?'

'Well, you know, commitment to Christ, recommitment to Christ, healing of the body – all that sort of thing.'

Suddenly felt terrified. Said in a feeble voice, 'I don't really do – ministry.'

Looked at me for a moment then said, 'No problem, I'll do it for you.'

Felt even more nervous after that. Not at all helped by the introduction Gary gave me when the worship had finished.

He said in a deep and thrilling voice, 'Friends, through the words of the man who's about to come to this microphone now, the Lord is going to change your lives, I can promise you that. Friends, he'll make you laugh. He'll make you cry. He'll bring the power and the light of God winging into the very centre of your hearts. Friends, as you leave this place tonight you will indeed know that you have been in the presence of the Most High. The justice of God and the love of God will be revealed to you in a wonderful way as this brother witnesses to the mighty twofold dispensation.'

Mentally abandoned my opening story about a vicar, a balloon and a mutant pineapple.

'Open your hearts, friends,' went on Gary, 'to receive the blessing you've craved for years. Please greet the messenger of God who stands before you now with sanctified lips and an anointed tongue.'

So nervous by now that when I *was* finally allowed to actually come to the microphone and I tried to speak, my sanctified lips and anointed tongue were too dry to produce anything but unintelligible sounds for a few seconds. Tempted to stop and wait in stern silence for an interpretation, but decided God wouldn't be very pleased.

Afraid my talk failed signally to live up to Gary's advance publicity. Mainly because I tried to make it do just that. There's something about people saying I'm going to witness to the mighty twofold dispensation that really glues up my delivery.

Finished my address hoping the gloomy silence was evidence of people being deeply moved. Don't think it was. More likely to have been evidence that I should have told the story about the vicar, the balloon and the mutant pineapple. Suddenly realized how stupid it was to be so affected by someone else's expectations. Sank miserably back in my seat and got on with dying quietly.

Gary wasn't put off in the slightest. Garys never are. Uncoiled himself in slow motion from his chair in that hushed, carefully-not-destroying-the-atmosphere sort of way, exuding significance from every pore, and spoke through the microphone in an even deeper and yet more thrilling voice than before.

'I'm sure you were as moved and challenged by that inspired word as I was, friends' – I'm quite sure they were – 'and I want to give you a chance now to respond to the touch of God on your heart. Don't leave here tonight, brothers and sisters, without doing business with the living God, I beg you.'

Suddenly became businesslike.

'Right! Our counsellors are ready. All those who want to make a first-time commitment to Christ, perhaps you could line up down here at the left-hand side of the stage. All those who want to make a recommitment to Christ, could I ask you to form a line down on my right-hand side? Those requiring healing of the body just queue down the middle between those two lines, and anyone who doesn't fit into any of those categories, perhaps you could form up by the steps over on my *far* right-hand side and beside the swing-doors on my *far* left-hand side if the numbers involved demand a second line.'

All very straightforward in theory, but it actually ended up with hundreds of people milling blankly around saying things like, 'Thing is – I want to make a recommitment, but I need healing of the body as well, so should I go in this line or that line, or the one over there?'

Whole thing began to feel like some badly organized divine carboot sale, with people wandering from line to line seeing what was on offer. Glad to get back to the hotel tonight. Told Anne all about the evening and asked why she thought I was feeling so guilty and unhappy.

She said without even pausing for thought, 'You're feeling guilty because you tried to do a Gary instead of an Adrian, and you're unhappy because you probably bored the socks off them in the process.'

I said, 'No, don't hold back, Anne, say exactly what you think.'

She said, 'I did.'

Perhaps I'll save the satire for my next book . . .

## Sunday 3 April

Spoke at an Anglican church this morning. Left Gerald and Thynn in their beds this time, and went with Anne. Funny how the events you dismiss as being trivial turn out to be the really meaningful ones. God seemed to be absolutely in charge of what I was saying for the half hour I was preaching.

Back to the vicarage afterwards for Sunday lunch. As we went in through the door, the vicar, whose name is Col Bevin, said very graciously, 'I believe you're bringing something very fragrant into our house today.'

He was right about me bringing something into the house, but I'm afraid it wasn't very fragrant. I brought it in on the sole of my shoe. We'd flopped gratefully into the soft, comfortable sitting-room chairs, and sherries were being poured, when Col's son, Jimmy, who's about fourteen, suddenly screwed up his nose and said, 'Blimey, Dad, someone's trod in something!'

Don't know why I assumed it couldn't be me. Something incongruous about delivering the word of God one moment and distributing dog poo over somebody's carpet the next, I suppose. You really would think that an interventionist God worth his salt might have done something about that, wouldn't you? An angel with a pooper-scooper or something?

Everyone except me was studying the soles of their shoes and sniffing round the room when Col's wife Noelene screamed and pointed to the piece of pale lilac carpet under and around my feet. It was covered in the stuff. That scream said 'NEW CARPET!' as clearly as if she'd used the words themselves. Anne was furious. Dragged my shoes bodily off my feet, hissing imprecations as she did so, and hurried out into the garden to clean them up. I jumped up and started hopping around making clicking noises with my tongue, hoping to express remorse through activity, pointless though the activity actually was. Col was determined not to make a big deal of it.

He said, 'No worries, Adrian, please don't distress yourself. Anyone could have done the same. A carpet is just a thing, and things can be replaced. We'd rather have your words this morning than a perfectly clean carpet, wouldn't we, Noelene?'

Noelene, who was already frantically at work on the carpet with a cloth and some kind of spray, forced a twisted smile onto her face, but I knew the real answer to her husband's question was:

'No, frankly, I would swop a carpet with no dog poo on it for the words he spoke this morning any day if such an exchange was an option, which it isn't. Furthermore, as you well know, this brand new *thing* has replaced the threadbare old *thing,* which I put up with for years and years and years. I would like him to feel free to distress himself as much as possible, thank you very much.'

Worked as hard as I could to redeem myself after that, talking to Jimmy about cricket, complimenting Col on the atmosphere in his church, and being utterly overwhelmed by the quality of the lunch, but it was no good. Poor Noelene was unable to prevent her eyes from continually drifting down towards my now poo-less shoes. I had sullied her pride and joy, and she just didn't trust me any more.

Said to Anne on the way home, 'Why is it that preaching and poo always seem to go together in my life?'

She replied rather coldly, 'Because you don't always look where you're walking.'

Hmmm ...

## Monday 4 April

Explosion in jumble sale repeated. Sad to be thinking of leaving, but excited to be going home.

## Tuesday 5 April

Anne, Gerald, Leonard and I entertained before leaving for the airport by *the* perfect Christian family.

Father warm and loving yet balanced and strong, mother clearly a perfect manager, yet flexible and fully involved with her children's lives, two beautiful teenage daughters alive and vibrant, yet sensible and self-disciplined, small boy endearingly mischievous, yet obviously good-hearted. *All* the children were polite but entirely natural, and all talked about deep experiences they'd had with God over the last few months. Everyone helped quite spontaneously with anything that had to be done, and there was not a single hissed threat, warning, bribe or entreaty from parents to offspring. To top all this, when we'd finished our snacks and drinks (prepared willingly by one daughter, served with humble elegance by the other, and passed assiduously by the little brother) the whole family *sang Christian choruses <u>in harmony</u> to us!*

A disgusting display altogether, in fact. We all felt obliged to role-play bubbling joy to match theirs. Very wearying. Tempted to pinch the small boy hard to make him swear or something. He'd probably have forgiven me, though ...

To make matters even worse they all insisted on treating me as if I was some kind of spiritual expert or guru. When the singing had finished the perfect father turned to me and said, 'My wife and I wondered if you would mind very much giving us the benefit of your wisdom and experience in a certain matter.'

Tried to ignore Gerald's sardonic eye and Thynn's look of blank puzzlement.

'Er, yes, of course, if there's anything I can help you with – of course.'

'Well, we know that your son –' he smiled in Gerald's direction, 'is grown up now, and often there will just be the two of you at home, but we were hoping that you could tell us which model of family worship you have used over the years.'

I said, 'Ah!', as if this were the very question I'd been longing for them to ask.

Anne and Gerald and I looked at each other. I asked a silent question. They answered in the affirmative without nodding or speaking. Sometimes loyalty embodies a greater truth than the truth itself.

I said, 'Ah, yes, family worship, yes. Which model . . . yes. Well, er . . . yes. Actually, we've always tried to be as flexible as possible with family worship –'

The perfect parents leaned forward, frowning and nodding interestedly, anxious to benefit from my great wisdom as much as possible while they had the chance. Any minute now they'd start taking notes.

'How exactly do you mean?' asked the perfect mother.

'Well, flexible in the sense that if anyone didn't want to come they didn't have to be there. And that er . . . that always worked out very well, because, generally speaking, none of us wanted to come so, er . . . we didn't.'

The whole perfect family fell about laughing at this point, clearly believing this unplanned moment of honesty to be a deliberate and hilarious joke on my part. No family worship time? What a rib-tickler! The perfect father patted me on the back while he chortled, as if I really was his sort of Christian-fun-chap. Taking the line of least resistance, Anne, Gerald and I laughed heartily with them (Thynn overdid it, of course, ending up rolling around on the floor), and then, thank goodness, it was time to go to the airport in their enormous, clean, perfect, rubbish-free Christian vehicle.

Whispered to Anne in the back of the car, 'Can't wait to be on our own so that we can be unholy in comfort.'

126

Called a final farewell some time later as we passed through the departure gate. The perfect family stood in a little shining group, still exuding love, joy, peace and harmless high spirits in every direction as they waved a vigorous goodbye to the departing spiritual guru and his lucky family and friend.

As soon as they were out of sight we all relaxed like four human balloons deflating.

Gerald said, 'Blimey! I've never been so relieved to get back into morose mode. The muscles in my face were beginning to ache with all that victorious smiling.'

Anne suddenly said, 'Look out! Bubbly smiles on! There they are again.'

Sure enough our erstwhile hosts had found their way round to a place from which they could see into the glass-walled walkway that led to the boarding gates. There they stood, smiling and waving as before. Instant resurrection in the Plass family. Thynn grinned like a maniac. We all waved back with guru-and-his-family-type smiles on our faces, then collapsed again with exhaustion as we passed on out of their sight.

Could feel my face crumpling into a visible groan. 'Oh, dear! I honestly don't think I could manage to get myself -'

'They're there again!' screamed Gerald, as we rounded the corner. 'I don't believe it! Look! They're there *again!* Smile to attention, everybody!'

With the mental ingenuity we should have expected from them, the perfect family had indeed found, and rushed to occupy, yet another point from which to salute us as we headed for the safety of our plane. You could tell they were *immensely* excited and happy about being able to give us such a wonderful and unexpected surprise. We produced another frenetic burst of robotic joy before continuing on our way. But we were broken people now. Our false smiles stayed glued to our faces as we stumbled defeatedly along. Who could tell when they might be needed? We were ready to believe that our persecutors were capable of appearing at any time and in any place.

Even after the plane had taken off and we were thousands of

feet in the air, I hardly dared look through the window beside me, in case, by some impossible but perfect means, the Australian Von Trapp family turned out to be standing happily on the wing, smiling and waving and singing choruses in harmony and reminding us that we were not a perfect family, all the way back to Heathrow airport.

If only they hadn't been so *nice* as well as everything else . . .

## Wednesday 6 April

All there ever has been or ever will be is this plane . . .

## Thursday 7 April

*3 p.m.*
Only an hour to Heathrow now.

Very relieved to have my diary to write just at this moment. Struck up a conversation a while ago with the very smart American lady sitting on my left. All right at first, but took a rather unfortunate turn after a while. Discovered as we talked that she's married to a very well known Christian speaker who I met for about three seconds at Let God Spring into Royal Acts of Harvest Growth a few years ago.

I said, 'Ah, yes, I know your husband well, he's a terrible man!'

She gave me a very straight look and said, 'He's not a terrible man – he's a very *good* man.'

Occurred to me that English irony might not be completely understood in the New World.

'I know,' I said, simpering and wriggling with embarrassment, 'that's what I meant. I was er . . . joking.'

She said slowly, and without even the ghost of a smile, 'I see – so when you said he was a terrible man, what you actually meant was that he's a good man?'

Cackled foolishly and said, 'Yes.'

Where is death when you really want it?

Now I know why nobody buys my books in America. I shall tell everyone the problem is that Americans just don't understand irony. That sounds much better than saying they don't find them funny.

### Friday 8 April

Forgotten how green England is. Can hardly write this, I'm so tired. Still, we did it, didn't we? Not sure who, what, when, where, how or why, but we did do it ...

### Saturday 9 April

Australia's just a dream. We never really went. Took our films in to the chemist so that we can prove we went. Should be ready on Monday.

Richard phoned, sounding very strained, to ask if his son Charles, who's visiting at the moment, could come to lunch or something next week. Anne's always got on well with Charles, so I expect Richard's hoping she'll talk to him about – what?

Anne said she'd ring Charles and ask him to eat with us on Monday evening.

### Sunday 10 April

Really good to be home.

Actually managed to get to church this morning. Walked in trying to look like someone who is hardly aware that others regard him with a certain awe because of his position as an international Christian speaker. When am I going to learn? Whole church distracted by talk of a new movement of the Spirit that apparently started in the Far East and is known as the Taiwanese Tickle. Whole thing appears to centre on fish! I gather Doreen Cook went off to some other church somewhere and – well, caught it, and brought it back.

Never seen anything like it. In the course of the service Richard Cook undulated around the hall like a very solemn eel taking bad news to someone, Elsie Burlesford – or Elsie Farmer, as I shall have to get used to calling her – flapped her arms like fins and made 'BOB' noises, and George Farmer leapt around energetically being a salmon travelling upstream. Lots of people fell on the floor, wriggling like happy sardines in a net and laughing out loud (presumably not at George Farmer). Young William Farmer conducted a time of healing at one stage. Lots of noise, but nobody seemed to actually be healed, as far as I could see. Didn't seem to bother William much. Presumably he got used to producing an opposite effect to the one intended when he was singing with Bad News for the Devil all those years ago. He certainly went happily back to doing lobster impressions after the prayer time. Hard to know what to make of it all.

At coffee time Gerald and Anne and I sat with Richard and Edwin. Richard asked us what we thought of the 'new wave'.

Gerald said, 'Richard, one very serious thought has occurred to me.'

Richard leaned forward and nodded encouragingly. 'Yes?'

'Well, it's going to be very tough on evangelists from Taiwan coming into this country, isn't it?'

'In what way?'

'Well, six months in an aquarium in quarantine is no joke if you're being a herring for the Lord, is it? I'd be gutted.'

Edwin chuckled, but Richard, unbelievably, said, 'You don't seriously think that will be a problem, do you?'

Anne told Gerald to stop being annoying and get some coffee for us all. Richard went to help with the carrying.

Anne said, 'Seriously, Edwin, what is it all about? It does look a bit odd when you walk into the middle of it like we did this morning.'

Edwin shrugged and smiled a little wearily. 'I'm glad you asked that, Anne. You know how it is. God starts something off and it's really good, then it gets – well, I suppose the word is hijacked, by some of us people in the churches, and we try to give it a shape and a name that it never really had, and then other people think we're the experts and copy our mistakes in a slightly different way, and more folk follow their lead until it's difficult to know if the thing you've ended up with is the same as the thing that God started in the first place. It's a bit like Chinese whispers. I mean – everything that's genuine in this "tickle" thing is originally from God, not from Taiwan, for goodness' sake.'

Wish I was like Edwin. Whenever he says anything vaguely critical he always talks about 'us' and never 'them'.

I said, 'You think it's from God – all the fish stuff?'

Edwin shrugged. 'Well, I do think God is anxious to bring a bit of lightness and relaxation into the business of being a Christian, and some people I know have had really wonderful experiences. I also think ...' Shifted his position and thought for a moment before going on – I love it when Edwin has things to say about things. 'I think a lot of Christians have got very disappointed over the last few years. So many promises in such fine, combative language about mighty works of revival and healing and goodness knows what other victorious events that are going to happen at any moment, and an awful lot of those promises don't seem to have been ful- filled – at least, not in the ways that people expected. There's a sort of weariness around, and I think maybe God, who is after all –'

'Very nice.'

'Yes,' smiled Edwin, 'fancy you guessing I was going to say that – God, who is definitely very nice, is probably offering us a kind of pick-me-up, which is great. And we should be able to han- dle some of the more er ... vivid manifestations without too much trouble. I think Elsie will –' He stopped and looked guardedly around the room. 'Where is she? Oh, good, she's right over there. I think Elsie will be starting on a diet of ants' eggs any day now. No, seriously, I welcome it and I'm wary of it, and I hope it helps people to see and accept that the real victories are a bit more costly and more local and more boring and more Jesus-like than a lot of these grand-sounding things that never quite happen. The hardest thing, Anne, when you're a twit like me, and you're sup- posed to be running a church, is working out how you get people to actually *do* things. They all want to laugh and cry and even be deeply moved as they watch the play, but not many want to be in it. I know I'm a bit old-fashioned, but I do prefer James' defini- tion of true religion to most other people's.' Suddenly clapped his hand to his head. 'Oh, dear – forgive me for rambling on like this. I've thought a lot about all this lately, and there aren't many people I can open up to.'

Pretty sure he was talking about Anne. She always makes people feel safe.

Richard and Gerald came back with the coffee. Gerald said, 'I was just asking Richard if he feels there can be salvation without salmon-leaping, but I've just remembered what Paul said on the subject.'

Edwin said, 'This should be interesting, to say the least.'

'There were three things,' said Gerald solemnly. 'First, the apostle enquires rhetorically, 'Do all leap like salmon?', and then, a little later in the same book, "I thank God that I leap like a salmon more than any of you", and again, 'The spirits of salmon-leapers are subject to the control of salmon-leapers".'

Short pause while Richard's brain double-declutched.

He said, 'I always thought those passages were about tongues.'

## Monday 11 April

Anne collected our films from the chemist today, and Leonard came round for lunch so that we could all look at them. Like peering through little bright windows at a different part of our lives. Hope we go back one day.

Charles Cook to dinner today.

Easy to see why Richard and (presumably) Doreen are so worried about him. Years ago, when he was studying at Deep Joy Bible College, Charles made Billy Graham look like a backslider. He wrote long, passionate, epistolary letters full of religious language, dire warnings and exhortations couched in vaguely prophetic tones to various members of the church. He wasn't just on fire for God – he was a human torch. In those days it was Gerald who took the mickey out of Charles (fortunately, Anne reckoned) and Charles who remained earnest and unremittingly spiritual regardless of what was being said or done around him at the time. Hardly seemed possible that the silly but rather engaging young man we'd once known could have altered quite so much. So floppy and cynical. Didn't seem capable of being anything but morose or sarcastic today. Even Anne, who used to get on really well with Charles, was obviously puzzled about the change that had come over him.

Compared notes afterwards and found that both of us were dying to ask what had happened to alter him so much, but didn't like to at first.

Not a little interested to find out how Gerald would react to someone who was in a much more sceptical state of mind than he had ever been. Quite pleased when he made a real effort to get Charles talking about a big Christian festival that Gerald loves and tries to get to every year. Charles has never been.

Gerald said, 'You'd love the huge open-air service at the end. It's completely non-denominational and unbiased. Ever so moving.'

Charles frowned. 'Oh, yes,' he said, 'I've heard about that service. You're right. It's completely undenominational and unbiased and free, except that – correct me if I'm wrong – it *has* to include somebody Scottish and impressively uncompromising teaching tunes and telling people off, and it's compulsory that there's a long, incomprehensible song written by a black, female, African, bi-sexual, disabled terrorist, and it's essential that there's a ten-minute section in which someone, preferably from the Middle East, shouts out great truths in a bellowing monotone. That's about it, isn't it? Oh, no, sorry, I missed out the fact that the liturgy has to be flexible enough to avoid excluding our brothers in the Tractor Worshipping Assembly of Northwestern Latvia, and particularly those members of that assembly (every single one of them, that is) who have never and will never, hear of, or have any connection with, the festival that strains so hard to accommodate their proclivities – very important point, that.'

Gerald completely nonplussed by all this. Later, Anne said that, over the years, Gerald has got into the habit of using Charles as a sort of symbol of silly Christianity, so it was no surprise that he couldn't handle the transformation that seems to have happened. Sounds a bit complicated to me, but Anne's probably right – she usually is.

Anne said, 'Now come on, Charles. You've never been. Honestly! How can you be so critical when you haven't got the first idea what you're talking about?'

'You ought to come one year, Mum,' said Gerald, grateful for the support, 'they had a whole series of banner-making seminars this year. Not quite my sort of thing, but you would've really enjoyed going to those.'

Anne and her friend Liz have made several beautiful banners for our church. Lots of people have said how much they add to the feel of the place. I never quite know what to think about them, but Charles seemed to have no doubt about his opinion.

'I've always thought,' he said, 'that – '

'You mean you've only just thought,' interrupted Gerald dryly.

'I've always thought that I'd like to lead a banner *ripping* seminar at a festival like the one you're talking about, Gerald. I'm sure an awful lot of people would turn up, don't you agree? I can just imagine it . . .'

Charles stood up, clapped his hands, and addressed us from the end of the table in those jolly, let's-have-a-good-time tones that one somehow associates with Christian workshops.

'Right, everybody, one or two still coming in, but I think we'll make a start. Can I ask everyone to just move into small groups of four or five, and what I want you to do is just share with each other as openly as you can – no pressure – the different reasons why you hate all these blinking silly banners that infest our churches, okay? And perhaps one person in each group wouldn't mind acting as a scribe – ha, ha! – so that you can write down what everybody says, and then, in about – ooh – five minutes, we'll have a time of reporting back and brainstorming and I'll just write it all up in black marker-pen on this big sheet of paper. Okay? Off you go into your small groups, and let's have you mixing with folks you don't know, so that you'll feel more uncomfortable, eh?'

Anne opened her mouth to say something, but Charles was in full, unstoppable, pseudo-jolly flow by now.

'Right, well, we've had our feedback session, and it's amazing, isn't it, folks, how we come to a session like this thinking that we're the only people in the world who hold the views that we do, only to discover that we all loathe banners for exactly the same reasons?

'Good! Now we come to the practical bit, and, look, please don't worry if you don't get the hang of it straight away. Just watch what someone else is doing and copy them and you'll be fine. After all, that's the way the church has worked for years, isn't it? Okay, well, if you look around you'll see that we've got scissors, we've got knives, we've got matches – do please use the sand-bins provided – and we've got a couple of little vats of acid for those who are into that, and, listen folks, there's absolutely nothing wrong with tearing the things to bits with your teeth and bare hands if that's the way you feel you're being led. Okay? So, I want a group of fifteen or so over here with the scissors – thank you. And let's have four or five on the knife table – good. A couple of volunteers for the acid? Great! And I'll lead a bigger group over on this side for the teeth and hand-tearing activity. And every time you hear this, folks,' Charles clapped his hands playfully, 'it's all-change time, okay? Ha, ha!

'Kids, no need for you to feel left out. As we destroy each banner we'll pass on the fragments to you, and Uncle Stan, who's over in the corner there wearing the Thompson's gazelle costume – cheer up, Uncle Stan? Isn't he great! – Uncle Stan will lead you in a time of jumping up and down on the remains.'

Raised his voice as if speaking over a busy hubbub of activity.

'Plenty of banners around, everybody – all absolutely sick-making. Some specially chosen because they were made in prophetic banner-making sessions – have a really good time with those. And, a final word, if you run out of puff – ha, ha! – or motivation, have a butchers at the list we've made, all the reasons why we loathe and despise the ghastly, flappy, banal objects, and I'm sure you'll feel a new surge of energy and commitment! Go for it, folks!'

Gerald smiled dutifully, but I could tell he didn't really find it funny. Well, it wasn't. It was full of anger and bitterness.

Somehow knew Anne wasn't going to let Charles go without making sure he knew how she felt. I was right.

Anne said, 'Charles, dear, what's happened to you?'

Isn't it funny when a person who's not being themselves knows exactly what another person's meant, but they have to pretend they don't understand the other person because they're so busy being this other kind of person who would never be able to understand what the other person meant.

(Read that last bit to Anne, and she said she knew what I meant, but didn't think anyone else would. Still, I'll leave it in.)

Charles said morosely, 'Nothing much. I get up, eat, go to work, come home, eat, watch telly, go to bed, sleep – then it starts all over again. I don't know what you mean by "happened". Nothing's happened to me.'

Anne said very gently, 'We've all known you ever since you were a little boy, Charles, and for most of that time your belief in God was the most important thing in your life. You talked about it all the time, you went away to college to study the Bible so that you could pass on your faith to other people more effectively, you wrote us long letters telling us what God was doing in your life down at Deep Joy College, or whatever it was called – I've still got those letters upstairs – and you actually went on to be assistant pastor at a church up near Gillingham, didn't you?'

Charles nodded, but just stared into his coffee cup without saying anything.

'And then,' went on Anne, 'after quite a short time, didn't you leave that job and get another one in a shop in the same town –'

'A newsagent's, wasn't it?' said Gerald.

'A newsagent's, that's right, and neither your Mum nor your Dad, nor us – although it's nothing to do with us really – nobody knows quite what went wrong.'

Anne waited for a moment, but Charles still said nothing. He seemed to be carrying out some very delicate surgical work with a spoon on the bottom of his cup. Decided it was about time I said something. Just a bit nervous because Anne always seems to have a sort of script ready written for her at times like this, and I don't. Didn't want to say the wrong thing.

'And then, Charles,' I said, 'today – you seem to want to make fun of everything anyone says about the Church, and there's something not quite right about – '

'Gerald always did,' mumbled Charles, looking up briefly from the operation he had been performing with such concentration. 'Edwin always laughed when Gerald said things. He said things about me and Dad sometimes.'

Anne and Gerald and I looked at each other helplessly. I opened my mouth and shifted around in my chair as if I had something useful to say but wasn't quite sure how to put it, hoping that Anne would get in before me with something that *was* useful. She did.

'Charles,' she said in a firm voice, 'there were times in the past when I could have cheerfully murdered Gerald.'

'Thanks, Mumsy,' murmured Gerald.

'Well, it's true! In your endless quest to be funny and clever you quite often went right over the top when you and Charles were younger. I suppose you don't remember referring to Charles' college as "the old Muppet factory", do you? And what about that New Year's church party when Charles' Dad asked you if you had assurance? Come on – what did you say to him?'

'Forgotten,' lied Gerald.

'You said, "Yes, I'm with the Woolwich", didn't you?'

'Well, yes, but – '

'And have you also forgotten your contribution to that meeting we had once to discuss what form the Easter service should take? You suggested, if I remember rightly, that a huge artificial chicken should be slid along a wire over the heads of the congregation, and when it reached the middle it would "lay" a large egg onto the centre aisle.'

'That's right,' I said, remembering, 'and the egg would burst open and Charles' Dad would step out dressed as a baby chicken and shout, "New Life!". Was that right?'

'You've left out the bit about releasing live chickens into the congregation,' said Gerald.

Charles said without smiling, 'And you've left out the bit about Dad asking where you'd get the chicken from.'

'The point I'm making,' said Anne, still sounding quite firm, 'is that you're right. Gerald has done a lot of mickey-taking when it comes to the Church, and sometimes he's done it thoughtlessly, and perhaps even ended up hurting folk from time to time. I don't defend that. But the things you've said today ...' Anne's voice softened as she went on. 'They're not the same, Charles. And I think the difference is – I think it's that Gerald always said what he said from *inside,* if you know what I mean. The things you're saying and the way you're saying them – well, they sound as if they're coming from someone who's right outside the Church – the *real* Church, as our friend Stephanie would hasten to remind us. So that's what my question meant, I suppose. What's happened to put you outside instead of inside? You're our friend, Charles, and we care about you –' Anne looked at Gerald and I '– don't we?'

We both nodded enthusiastically.

'I let go of the rope,' said Charles, in such a quiet voice that we had to strain to listen, 'and no one caught me.'

Somehow conquered the desire to say, 'What rope? Who didn't catch you?' There was quite a long silence, then Anne spoke.

'Charles, do you remember when you were in the middle of your college course and you decided to give it all up because the Lord was calling you to Israel?'

Gerald and I glanced at each other, exchanging an unspoken agreement that neither of us would laugh. On the occasion Anne was referring to, Charles had announced with great earnestness that every time he opened his Bible there seemed to be some reference to Israel, and that he felt this was a sign that he should abandon his course and head for the Middle East. Anne had seemed to know, as if by magic, that that wasn't really the problem at all, and everything seemed to get sorted out in the end.

Charles nodded sadly into his mug. 'Wish I had given it up then. Would've saved a lot of trouble.'

Anne said, 'But do you remember what it was that really helped on that particular evening? There was one of God's gifts that brought at least a glimmer of light into the darkness, wasn't there? Actually, it's something that always helped you from when you were a little boy.'

Charles looked up at Anne, curious despite himself. I was curious as well. What was she talking about? Prayer? Counselling? A particular verse from the Bible, perhaps?

'What was it, then?' asked Charles.

Anne opened the cupboard behind her and took out a large round tin. 'Cake,' she said, 'and especially chocolate cake.'

A little public smile trespassed on the surface of poor old Charles' private misery for just a moment. 'I do still like cake,' he said.

All munched for a while.

'You believe everything your Mum and Dad tell you when you're little, don't you?' said Charles a minute or so later. 'My Mum and Dad made me believe that you ought to feel excited and strong and hearing God all the time and – oh, I don't know – like them, I suppose. And for years and years I tried as hard as I could to at least look as if that was how I really was inside. I tried ever so *hard,* you know ...'

A tear plopped into the coffee mug with a surprisingly loud sound. We ate cake and passed tissues and waited.

'I learned how to pray and sing choruses and quote bits from the Bible and do all the things that Christians are supposed to do, and, looking back, I can see that I was making a real idiot of myself. Because it was never really happening inside, you see. I didn't feel Jesus in me or any of that. I wasn't H-A-P-P-Y, or whatever it was we used to sing. I was P-A-N-I-C-K-Y. I wondered how long it would be before this God that Mum and Dad talked about all the time noticed what an effort I was making and showed himself to me in some way and *made* it all real. That's what I meant about the rope just now. It got more and more difficult to pretend. It was like dangling over some awful pit, hanging on to the end of a rope by one hand like grim death, terrified that, at any moment, I'd let go and fall. But a bit of me ... A bit of me hoped that if – when – I did let go, God would sort of catch hold of me and take me somewhere safe. But he didn't. As soon as I started the job in Kent I knew it wasn't going to be any good. You can't go round door-to-door trying to sell something you haven't got, can you? I couldn't anyway.'

Gerald said, 'What's in this pit of yours, Charles – the one you've landed in?'

'My Dad's disappointed face mainly,' said Charles miserably. 'I know Dad's a bit of a twit sometimes.' (Gerald blushed faintly,

139

I'm pleased to say.) 'But he's always been – he's always cared a lot about what happens to me, and he was so excited when I went to college, and then when I got the job. I knew Mum and Dad would never really be able to understand what's happened to me because they're not made like that. Dad especially just *knows* everything about God is true and all right, and that's that. He really does – he's not kidding. The thing about Dad is that if he finds out he's wrong about something he'll change it, even if he's been going on and on about it in the wrong way for ages. He means it all, you see. So, even if I told him that all that trying had really been for him I don't think he'd have the faintest idea what I was talking about. And if he did understand he'd be so upset and guilty that I couldn't stand it. That's why I stayed up there and found a job after leaving college. I couldn't face seeing that puzzled, hurt, wanting-to-do-the-right-thing look on his face all the time.'

Anne said, 'So that's where all the anger's coming from, Charles – the feeling that God's let *you* down, and you've let your Dad down and everything's just ghastly?'

'More or less,' replied Charles, then, trustingly, like a small child, 'What shall I do, Anne?'

'There are two things I want to say to you, Charles,' said Anne. 'First, I think that all of us here in this room owe you an apology, don't we, Adrian?'

Rather taken by surprise.

'Er, yes, yes, certainly we owe you an – an apology, Charles, for – well, for er . . . obvious reasons.'

'You mean about the past, Mum?'

Anne smiled. 'Yes, Gerald, about the past. I don't know what's the matter with us Christians. We're so busy being civilized that we forget to be helpful, don't we?'

I nodded gravely, and said, 'True, true.' Hadn't got even the remotest idea what Anne was talking about.

'The thing is, I could have told you years ago that this was likely to happen one day, Charles, but I didn't, because it – well, it's pathetic I know, but it didn't seem to be any of my business. I could see you desperately trying to be what your parents wanted you to be, and if I'd had a bit more courage, or whatever it needed, I'd have told you that's not the same as being a Christian, and maybe saved you at least a bit of all this pain. I'm really sorry. It seems to have always been a problem in our sort of church that as long as people are making the right kind of noises we just let them get on with it, even when we're quite sure there's a real vacuum underneath. Please forgive me – us – for letting you down like that.'

'Course I do, Anne,' said Charles. 'It wasn't your fault anyway. You've always been kind to me. What – what was the other thing you wanted to say?'

'Just that I think you're underestimating your father. Just at the moment I don't think it matters a jot what you believe or don't believe. You're far more worried about it than God is – if he exists, that is, of course. I think your Dad would handle actually knowing what's going on far better than he's coping with worrying and guessing. Why don't you just tell him? I think you'd be surprised.'

'Just tell him?'

'Mm.'

Charles always was like a little doggy with Anne. He got straight on to the phone and asked his Dad to come round to our house because he'd got something to say to him. Poor old Richard was knocking on the door within minutes, his face a mask of tension and worry when I let him in. We left the two of them alone in the kitchen and waited in the sitting-room for what seemed like hours. When father and son emerged at last – well, talk about two little rays of sunshine! Richard didn't know where to put himself, he was so pleased. He fiddled excitedly with the inevitable tie around his neck as he spoke.

'Charles has er, explained some of the er, problems that he has er, faced over the past few years, and I am so pleased that he has told me about – told me about – well, told me about them. I feared that he might simply be angry with me for being – for being – well, for being me, I suppose, but I'm quite sure now that we shall be able to . . .'

Richard scratched his head, clearly not quite able to express what it was that they would be able to do, but it didn't matter. I think we knew what they meant. They knew they loved each other and that wasn't a bad beginning.

Came across Gerald in the kitchen much later, laughing quietly to himself. Asked what he was finding so funny.

He said, 'Oh, I was just thinking about old Charles' banner ripping seminar. It may be a very negative concept, but, you know, I think he was probably right. An awful lot of people would turn up . . .'

Found myself thinking about the Cooks just before settling down for the night. Why did Charles hardly mention his mother? Why didn't she come round with Richard?

## Tuesday 12 April

Can't bear the thought of going back to work next week. I know it's awful, but I feel as if Glander's a sort of blockage in my main pipe. Disgusting image, I know, but that's how it feels.

## Wednesday 13 April

Prayed with Anne about Glander at lunchtime today. The whole thing's filling my mind in the most ridiculous way. Anne says we must trust God now that we've prayed, but my experience is that he hardly ever does exactly what I want in exactly the way that I want him to do it.

## Thursday 14 April

*11:00 a.m.*

Tremendously excited and tremendously annoyed and all sorts of other things by a phone call from Everett Glander just now. The only time in my life I can remember God replying by first post.

Conversation began as follows:

'Adrian? Glander here – Everett Glander. How was Oz?'

'Oh, fine, thanks, Everett. Had a great time, yes. It really went well. How are you?'

'Well, have you got a minute? I know you international speakers are terribly busy.'

'Don't be silly – yes, of course, what can I do for you?'

Always get very tense when Glander phones. Find myself clenching my teeth and plucking nervously at the telephone wire. Why on earth would he be ringing from work on a Thursday morning? I wasn't supposed to be back, was I?

'Well, the thing is, old man – hold your hat – I think I've become one of them – or rather, one of you.'

'Become one of me? What do you mean?'

'I mean I've become one of your lot, old man. I've joined – taken the King's shilling. I am of the elect. You and I are little brother sunbeams.'

Pause while it sunk in.

'Is what you're trying to tell me that *you* have become a *Christian*, Everett?'

'Well, that's about the size of it, chief, and I must say I feel pretty damn good. Wish I'd taken the plunge years ago.'

Glander made it sound like joining a swimming club, but I suppose that's just his way. The thing that really bothered me was the conflict in my own reactions to this news. Part of me was very pleased – of course – but, despite my prayer of yesterday, another part of me was horrified. Everett has always managed to diminish me in my own eyes. Everything that I've thought worth anything seems to shrink and feel silly when I'm with him. What's it going to be like if he's in our church or even in our Bible-study group? What if – heaven preserve me! – what if Edwin decides that Glander is a candidate for my support group? The thought of him sitting there listening to intimate things about me and then making his caustic comments in front of everyone else just makes my blood run cold.

Tried to respond as enthusiastically as I could. Not easy.

'Well, that's terrific news, Everett! A real surprise.'

'You mean you're surprised that a black-hearted pagan like me has enough strength left in his sin-raddled body to drag himself up to the mercy seat, old man?'

'No, of course I didn't mean that. I just meant – I don't know what I meant,' I finished lamely. 'Anyway, tell me how it happened.'

'Well, I guess there must have been statues running blood and ladybirds coming to life in children's tee-shirts and signs in the sky and sundry other portents all over the place last Friday if one had but known where to look, because it all happened by chance, saving his presence, if you know what I mean.'

'What happened?'

'Went for a couple of jars at the King and Country as is my wont on a Friday night, and on the way back – you know that little old-fashioned chapel-type place set back between the Q8 garage and the Chinese takeaway?'

'Yes, but they're not really what I'd call – '

Suddenly stopped as I realized what I was saying. In the past, I'd tended to dismiss the church Everett was talking about as being dowdy and lifeless. Now I realized I didn't know anything about it at all.

'Not what you'd really call what, old man?'

'Oh, I just meant I've never actually been there, that was all.'

One of the things that's always frightened me about Glander is the way he seems to be able to see behind what I've said and then comment on it. That's what he did now.

'Well, that's a great relief, old chap. I thought for one dreadful moment you were going to say that they were some sort of spiritual lowlife down there. You weren't going to say that, were you?'

'Er, no, of course not.'

'Oh, good. Anyway – where was I? Oh, yes, on the way back from the hostelry I just happened to notice that there was some sort of knees-up going on in this little chapel place and I sort of drifted through the door and slotted in at the back while they were singing. Tried not to breathe on anyone – fruit of the hop must have wafted out on the wings of 'Shine Jesus Shine', I fear. And then this bloke did a talk. Didn't appear all that promising at first I have to say. In fact, you know they sometimes reproduce those little Edwardian books with pictures that told you what to wear and how to comb your hair and behave properly in company?'

'Yes, I – I think I know the sort of thing you mean.'

'Well, this character reminded me of the pictures they put in to show you how it *shouldn't* be done. Norman Wisdom without cap or jokes – that's about the nearest I can get to it.'

'But it was a good talk?'

It was the first silence since the beginning of the phone call, but I could almost hear Everett struggling to find a way of saying something without wrapping it up in flippancy like coloured cellophane.

'Not so much a good talk. Just that – it suddenly all made sense.'

'What made sense?'

Rather enjoyed pressing Glander to make him say something he really meant.

'You know, all the stuff about going home – all the old prodigal stuff. That's what this geezer was on about, going home and everything being good – being forgiven. All that. Collared the bloke afterwards and asked him to come back to the King and Country with me. Bit of a challenge, I suppose. Blow me down if he didn't do exactly that. Tell you what, old man, if you haven't sat in the public bar of a working men's pub, with darts and farts and filthy jokes flying all round your head, listening to a Norman Wisdom lookalike talking about religion, you just haven't lived.'

'What did this man say that you hadn't heard already, then?'

'What *didn't* he tell me that I'd never heard, you mean. All the meaty stuff about being a new man in Christ, for a start.'

'But I told you – '

'And then there was the link-up between the Old Testament and the New Testament. All those bullseye prophecies, old man. Amazing!'

'But I explained – '

'And just the fact that little old me, E. Glander himself, is a bit of a twinkle in the boss's eye. Never even guessed at it.'

'I can't remember how many times I tried to tell you – '

'Most important of all, though, old man, is that I can actually get it together, have what you'd call a real relationship with this Jesus of yours – mine – ours, I should say.'

'I can't *believe* you don't remember – '

'I must say, old man, I think you could've filled me in on a few of these bits of info before now.'

Felt ever so cross. All those years of listening to Glander's cynical comments and trying to tell him what my faith was all about, and in the end God sends Norman Wisdom along to tell him things he's already heard, and convert him in a pub.

'Went home after that,' continued Everett, 'and told the wife I wanted to sign up with "Big J", and she did a total dissolve on me. Cried all over the carpet, then said she'd been waiting for this to happen for years. She was way ahead of me.'

Felt very guilty suddenly. I suppose the Holy Spirit can do what he likes, when he likes. Well, I mean, of course he can. Tried to be more positive.

'Well, this is great news, Everett, it really is. I suppose you and Joyce will be going along to the chapel on Sunday, will you?'

Prayed silently that he would say yes.

'Good heavens, no, old man! We'll be coming to your place, of course. Wouldn't go anywhere else. That's the other reason I rang. Do you think Edwin, your elder fellow, would let Joyce and me do a little public announcement up front if I kept it shortish? Just to make it stick, as it were.'

Said I was sure Edwin would be pleased to let them do that, and promised to ring him myself and fix it up.

Everett said, 'Oh, one last thing – something else happened last night that I haven't told you or even Joyce about – '

'A spiritual experience, you mean?'

'Oh, yes, definitely one of those, old man, a real clincher, it was, but I think I'll keep it as a surprise for Sunday.'

Put the phone down with a rather heavy heart. Everett Glander is going to become a member of my church. Real life sticking its nose in again where it's not wanted.

Told Anne and Gerald what had happened at lunchtime. Gerald was too deeply buried in the paper to take much notice, but Anne received the news with genuine joy, as I thought she might.

She said, 'I'm so glad for Joyce, she's been so patient. I wouldn't have been able to stand the man all this time.'

'You don't mean he's even more annoying than me, do you?'

'No,' said Anne, who never indulges my fishing exploits, 'just annoying in a different and even less acceptable way.'

Explained to her how galling it was that Everett had heard all those things from Norman Wisdom about Christianity as if they were completely fresh, even though I'd been saying them to him on and off for years.

She said, 'I think you're underestimating the effect you've had on him over the years, darling. It's like the old Chinese water torture, isn't it? A little drop falling at regular intervals has an enormous impact over a long period, I'm quite sure. Why don't you suggest to Edwin that you interview Everett and Joyce in church on Sunday, seeing as you know him better than anyone else.'

Thought the use of the Chinese water torture as a metaphor for my Christian witness was a little ill-chosen, but I see what Anne means. And I really like the idea of me interviewing them. Can't help hoping that people will see Everett and Joyce as fruits of my long-term labours, as it were. Maybe Everett won't be such a pain now that he's a Christian – have to wait and see. I wonder what this 'something else that happened' was. Quite looking forward to Sunday now.

As I was leaving the table, Gerald suddenly looked up from his newspaper with a puzzled expression on his face and said, 'Dad?'

'Yes?' I said.

'Was I imagining it, or did I hear you say just now that Everett Glander has been converted by Norman Wisdom in a pub?'

'That's right,' I said casually, enjoying not explaining.

'Is that meant to be a joke?'

'A joke?' I said lightly. 'Everett Glander being converted by Norman Wisdom is no funnier than – let me see – well, no funnier than you saying my attempt to mend Percy's roof was a futile gesture. Or perhaps just about as funny as that.'

Very seldom I defeat my son.

He sighed and said, 'All right, Dad, you explain Everett Glander and Norman Wisdom in the pub, and I'll tell you why your futile gesture made everyone laugh.'

Agreed.

He told me.

Well, now I know! It really wasn't worth waiting for. Certainly not worth entering for a decent horse race ...

Rang Edwin this evening to suggest the interview. He's known Everett on and off for a few years now, so he was really pleased to hear what had happened. Agreed enthusiastically with Anne's idea that I should ask Everett and Joyce a few questions – sort of draw them out, but thought I should phone them first to check that they were happy to do it that way. Phoned Everett straightaway and asked if he minded being interviewed.

He said, 'Joyce'll be a bit nervous, I should think, so go easy, old boy, won't you? But, yes, by all means do a Wogan on us – spot of kudos for you there, eh, old man?' How does he *always* know? 'Just so long as you don't forget to ask me about this other experience of mine, okay?'

Must jot a few questions down before the weekend. I really am quite intrigued by this 'other experience'. Roll on Sunday!

## Friday 15 April

Photocopies of two magazine reviews of my last book arrived in the post this morning, sent by someone at the publishers. Decided to prove Anne and Gerald wrong about my so-called inability to accept criticism. I shall read the first one now, and then comment on it in my diary, being as objective and mature as possible in my response.

## five minutes later

Well, I must say, this first piece is a fine, balanced piece of work. In style, structure and general presentation it can hardly be faulted. Here is a man or woman, one feels, with whom one would like to establish a warm personal friendship. Through the very words that are written the author seems to reach out to you, the reader, to say, 'You are safe with me – relax and trust me to lead you into paths of perception that will stimulate and enrich you.' Very impressed indeed. It is true that the specific comments contained in the review are almost all very pleasingly positive, but I honestly do believe that I would have arrived at the same conclusion if the general content had been negative.

Now I shall read the second review in exactly the same spirit of calm, unbiased objectivity.

### ninety seconds later

I'm sorry, but what's the point of trying to be objective when you're presented with garbage like this? I mean, if they really do insist on having reviews in this sad little rag of theirs, they might at least make sure that the person doing the review (a) is a human being who knows what a sentence is, and (b) has actually read the book he's supposed to be reviewing. It makes me want to vomit, it really does! Jumped-up, arty-farty drip of a person, I have no doubt, who's never written a book in his life, being allowed to comment publicly on the product of somebody else's hard work. Miserable parasite should be shot! Love to do it myself. Sod!

### Saturday 16 April

Meant to tear yesterday's entry out before Anne and Gerald got a chance to see it. Forgot! Rushed down this morning, but it was too late. Gerald's threatening to frame it and give a copy to all our friends as an Easter present.

### Sunday 17 April

Woke up this morning with that funny feeling you have when you know something's going to happen but you can't quite remember what it is, and you know you're either looking forward to it very much or absolutely dreading it, but you're not sure which. Mind you, once I *had* remembered what it was I still wasn't sure.

Felt quite good by the time I got to church, though. Looking forward to modestly facilitating a public demonstration of what the Lord can do through his battle-worn servants. Just a little concerned that Glander might reveal one or two of the less admirable excesses of this particular battle-worn servant. Decided to make sure the questions avoided any chance of him commenting on me.

Everett and Joyce had been given seats on the front row by Edwin, and they were already there, Joyce looking glowingly happy but darting little nervous glances around her all the time, and Everett relaxedly leaning his elbows on the back of his chair, just as he's always done at work.

Got a bit impatient during the early part of the service. Someone got up to bring us one of those 'thoughts' that always make me want to beat up the thinker. Such a nuisance, because then you wish you hadn't reacted like that and you feel you ought to repent and – oh, it all gets so tedious. This time it was Sadie Wingford, who's soupily devout and dresses like Alice in Wonderland even though she's in her mid-twenties. She jumped out of her seat just as we were about to sing one of my favourite choruses (the one that goes to the tune of 'Danny Boy'), and daisy-chained her way up to Edwin at the front, who listened with his usual patience as she whispered something in his ear.

Edwin said, 'Sadie's asked if she can share a thought with us, everybody. It's all yours, Sadie – away you go.'

'Well,' said Sadie in her breathless voice – Gerald says it makes her sound like a cross between Snow White and Marilyn Monroe – 'I just had a sudden precious little thought last night, and – well, it just seemed too beautiful to be kept to myself, so I said to the Lord, "Pretty please, can I share it with all my brothers and sisters at church tomorrow morning?" and he said, "Oh, yes!!". Who wants to hear my special thought?'

She cocked her head on one side, swivelled her eyes skyward and opened her mouth to the size of a golf ball, like someone listening for an echo on a mountainside in one of those bad musicals. The congregation stirred uneasily and produced a sort of assenting mumble. Interpreting these wretchedly uncomfortable murmurings as an enthusiastically positive response to the prospect of hearing her special thought, Sadie continued.

'My little thought was this. Isn't the Good News of the Gospel just like jam?'

'Oh, God!' groaned Gerald irreverently beside me in a whisper, 'I don't think I can stand hearing why the Good News of the Gospel is just like jam. Have I got time to get to the lavatory?'

He hadn't.

'The Good News of the Gospel is just like jam because –' Sadie paused dramatically, 'it needs to be SPREAD!!!'

Gerald suggested grimly that Sadie Wingford was just like cod because she needed to be battered. He was only joking, but I know what he means. She's very annoying at times.

Much more enjoyed a thought that Edwin told us he'd had.

He said, 'I came across a Bible verse that might possibly be a great encouragement to those ladies in the congregation who are not yet married, but would like to be. It's the first verse of psalm fifty-six: "Be merciful to me, O God, for men hotly pursue me ..."'

Raised quite a laugh around the church, including a rather raucous guffaw from Everett Glander at the front. Leaned across and said to Anne, 'Hope to goodness he really is redeemed.'

At last the time came for me to interview Everett and Joyce. Edwin invited us all up to the front without saying what was going to happen then sat down on the front row to listen.

Suddenly felt really good. Told everybody how I'd worked with Everett for a good few years and always longed that he might one day become a Christian (didn't actually mention how extremely irksome I'd found him for most of that time, nor that I'd rather hoped he would die when he had a cold recently). Went on to say that Everett had phoned me the other day with some good news and that he and Joyce wanted to share it with the congregation today.

(Isn't it funny how you slip into role on these occasions without even thinking about it. Gerald told me this evening that I was displaying all the bobbing, hand-washing, bottom-lip-between-the-teeth-grinning mannerisms that I'd noticed in others when they're doing similar things. 'Ah, well,' I said to him, 'don't suppose it really matters.' He said, 'No, as long as you're insincere. That's what counts.' Perhaps I misheard him.)

Glander explained with surprising simplicity about events at the chapel and the pub afterwards, and then I asked Joyce to tell everyone what had happened when he came home. People really warmed to Joyce, who is a slight, neatly dressed lady with a quiet voice, as she talked about how drawn to Jesus she had been for a long time, but how she'd more or less kept it to herself because she knew that Everett would not only be unable to handle it, but would probably have been driven even farther away from believing if he'd known. She nearly cried, but not quite.

One tricky bit just after Joyce had finished, when Everett said that working with me all these years must have had something to do with what had happened, despite, as he put it, 'one or two things that I'd better not mention'. My heart was in my mouth for a moment, thinking he was going to describe the awful occasion when I drank more than was good for me at the office party and told Everett to 'stuff his beliefs' after he'd told me yet again that he didn't agree with mine.

But he didn't, and I was beginning to feel a very satisfactory, warm, proprietorial glow about the whole thing. This man who had been a colleague of mine for all those years was standing beside me in church confessing his faith in Jesus. What a privilege!

'Don't forget, old man,' whispered Everett, interrupting my bask, 'you were going to ask me about my experience last night.'

My big mistake at this point was, of course, in deliberately giving the impression that I knew what he was about to say. I'd just got a bit carried away with the old proprietorial bit, I suppose.

What I actually said was, 'Ah, right! Everett's got one other thing to say, everybody, and I can tell you that this is quite something. The Lord has really been working in his life. Tell people what happened, Everett,' and I smiled, as if recalling some earlier account of whatever the occurrence had been.

'Right,' said Everett, 'well, folks and folkesses, I guess this was the icing on the old cake, as it were, and I want to say a big public

thank you to – well, I suppose I shall have to call him God from now on, won't I? Not that I didn't call him God before, you understand – I just didn't er – thank him for anything.'

I have to admit that it was good to see Glander floundering for once. I rather enjoyed being kind.

I said, 'Okay, Everett, take your time, old chap. Just relax and tell everyone how the Lord spoke to you.'

'Well, to be honest, old man,' said Everett, 'it wasn't so much the Lord who actually spoke to me – more my dead grandmother.'

Totally paralysed for a moment. Dead grandmother? We didn't allow dead grandmothers in our fellowship – not ones that spoke to their live grandsons anyway. What did he think he was doing? Decided I'd have to stop him somehow. Glander's voice is a very difficult one to stop, though. I writhed inwardly with embarrassment as he went on.

'Fact of the matter is, I always had a bit of a thing about old Granny, who, interestingly, was very much into the old Jesus stuff herself. You see, not having anything approximating to what you might call parents around for most of my natural born, I sort of depended on old Granny. Used to troddle down to Newhaven most weekends to check out this or that. She'd say what she thought, then I'd say thank you very much but I think you're probably wrong, then she'd smile in a way she had, then I'd go off home and find she was absolutely right. So, when, after all these years of being pummelled at work by our resident poor man's Billy Graham here (prolonged laughter from congregation – thank you, Everett), this funny business at the chapel and down the old Kings happened, everything in me said, "Glander, before you finally pop the parcel in the post, as it were, get yourself down to Newhaven and check it out with Granny." Stupid thing for Everything In Me to say, of course, because poor old Granny popped her clogs half a decade ago. Still – '

There was a pause as Everett's glasses steamed up a little. Joyce moved closer and took his arm. Here was my opportunity to stop this before it went any further.

'Well, on behalf of everyone here, Everett, I'd really like to thank you and Joyce for being so – '

'Hold on, old man,' said Glander, 'I haven't had a chance to tell everyone what happened yet.'

I peered ostentatiously at my watch before clicking my tongue against my teeth and sighing, as though deeply disappointed.

'It really does seem as if time's beaten us,' I said desperately, 'and I'm sure Edwin would agree that it's very important to – to stick to the timing that people are expecting – wouldn't you, Edwin?'

Threw an intense look at Edwin on the front row, a look which was designed to communicate, in that split second, the following:

*'Have you understood, as the elder of this church, that the lunatic standing next to me, this mega-annoying person who has made my life miserable at work for more years than I care to remember by pulling just this kind of stunt, is about to support his claim to conversion by describing some kind of conversation with an elderly person who's been dead since the mid-eighties?*

*Do you realize that one or two people here will almost certainly attempt to deliver him on the spot if he goes on much longer? Will you please, please agree with me that we haven't got time for any more?'*

I am quite sure that Edwin interpreted my burning stare with total accuracy, but he wasn't having any of it.

'No, you're okay for a while, Adrian,' he called out casually. 'In any case, I'm quite sure lots of people will be more than happy for me to lop five minutes of dead wood off my talk so that we can have a bit more of Everett's green stuff. You just carry on, Everett – plenty of time.'

'Yes, carry on, Everett,' I echoed limply, adding under my breath, 'with your heresy.' There was nothing else I could do.

'Ta muchly,' said Everett, adding slightly tartly, 'be nice to just finish. So, anyway, last night, after Joyce had gone up the wooden hill and I'd finished locking the cat and feeding the front door, as I always say, I thought I'd just sit in the dark for a second or two in Granny's old basket-chair in the corner of the sitting-room, and have a little think about what she'd have said if she could have seen Joyce and me actually praying together earlier.' He shrugged. 'Couldn't really say if I actually dropped off or not. Might have done, but it doesn't matter a row of beans when you come right down to it. I just seemed to see old Gran's face right there in front of me, and the thing of it is – well, Gran was smiling and nodding like she used to, and she said "yes". And that seemed to put the cap on the whole thing. I say,' he suddenly said to me, sensing my reaction as usual, 'I'm not embarrassing you by going on about Granny, am I? You haven't got the Spanish Inquisition hiding inside the lectern ready to jump out and torture people who talk about their deceased grandparents, have you?'

I stood there speechless, my mouth opening and shutting like an insulted guppy. Edwin rescued me by getting up and coming to the front to take over. Standing between Everett and Joyce with his arms around their shoulders, he said, 'I'm sure we'd all want to thank both of you for being brave enough to stand up here this morning so that we could hear about Jesus calling you to follow him. We're so glad that you're part of us now. As for that wonderful experience of seeing your grandmother last night – well, God is very good and very wise. My guess, Everett, is that you probably did doze for a while in that chair, and that God let you see in a dream the sort of reaction you'd have got if there was still someone down in Newhaven for you to go and see. He knew you needed to see that. In fact, I'm sure that's exactly how she is reacting in the place where she is now. Let's welcome Everett and Joyce, everybody.'

As I joined in the applause, I thought, yet again, of the way in which Edwin's personal faith and set of beliefs have a sort of elastic quality. Sometimes he seems to let them stretch to accommodate a person, or something a person thinks or says, but they never go out of shape. They always come back to where they started in the end, and at least one good thing usually happens in the process. Wish I was like that. Perhaps I will be one day.

Couldn't help feeling a certain satisfaction at seeing Stephanie Widgeon bear hungrily down on Everett as the service ended, presumably to share for the first, and hopefully by no means the last time, her novel insight into the nature of the Church.

Said to Anne this evening, 'The thing that worries me a bit is that the Spanish Inquisition wasn't hiding inside the lectern – it was hiding inside me.'

Anne looked up from what she was doing and said, 'Why don't you concentrate on being forgiven, and let God concentrate on being perfect?'

## Monday 18 April

Must remember to look up 'cleistogamic' in the dictionary.

## Tuesday 19 April

Horrific scene with Doreen this evening.

First of all Richard phoned, almost incoherent, to say that Doreen was on her way to see Anne and me, and that she was, as he put it, in a 'strongly rebuking mood'. Fact is, she was just plain seething. Refused anything to drink and wouldn't sit down. I asked her why she was so angry.

She looked at Anne as she replied, 'My son came to you in need of Christian counsel and you – you supported him in his sin and in his backsliding.'

'Doreen,' said Anne gently, 'I honestly don't think – '

'Did you tell him – ' Doreen raised her arm and pointed at Anne like some Old Testament prophet declaring judgment on Israel, 'that what he believes or does not believe is of no consequence?'

Anne shook her head in frustration. 'Yes, but it was – '

'Did you encourage Charles to believe that the Lord is unconcerned with his sin of doubt, and did you –' Doreen's face was suffused with colour as her voice lifted almost to a shout, 'did you yourself cast doubt on the very existence of God? Did you lead him to believe that all his past experiences were meaningless because they really meant something else, something that *you* should never have allowed to happen? Did you do that?'

'Doreen, that's a distortion of what really happened. I wanted Charles to relax so that his feelings about his father could – '

'You wanted! You wanted! You wanted! Why is what you wanted important? Tell me why the things you say and think and – *want,* have always been so much more important to my son than what I want. Why? Tell me why that is! I rebuke you in the name of the Lord for the way in which you have seduced him in the direction of your own ungodly liberalism and half-hearted adherence to the things of the Spirit and the word of God!'

This, obviously, was the speech that Doreen had been rehearsing on the way over to our house, and I have to admit that it left me quite speechless. I had a vague notion that, as the head of the household, I ought really to do something, but I couldn't think what to say. I needn't have worried. Anne suddenly stopped looking distressed and directed a very steady gaze towards Doreen. She spoke with a calm assurance that I've rarely heard, and, as she went on speaking, her voice was like the sound of a bell.

'There is nothing liberal about coming down the road that another human being is travelling, to meet them and bring them to safety. If that is liberal, then God is a liberal. There is nothing liberal about helping people to smash the false gods and images of religion or worldliness that have let them down and given them nothing over the years. If doing that is liberal, then God is a liberal. There is nothing liberal about using divine gifts of creativity and flexibility and ingenuity to open doors of understanding and delight in those who desperately need to know that compassion and care really are waiting for them in the arms of the Father. If that is liberal then the God who created this world is a liberal. There is nothing liberal about treading the narrowest path imaginable yourself, but throwing your arms as wide as they'll go to greet and enfold as many others as possible. If that is liberal, then all the most godly men and women I've ever known are liberals. There is nothing liberal, Doreen, about staying at the back of the expedition to tie shoelaces, and to encourage the fat ones and the slow ones and the ones whose feet hurt, rather than pushing triumphantly to the front of the line so that you can be first to the ultimate destination. If doing that is liberal, then Jesus was the greatest liberal of them all.'

There was a pause, and when Anne spoke again her voice was much softer.

'Doreen, I know you're really hurting, and I know a lot of it's to do with feeling that Charles isn't turning to you when he's so needy. If I've ever, in any way, made that worse, then I apologize without reserve, but don't you think that if you just – if you were to just freely offer him your love and support without worrying too much about the Christian side of things, just for a while – don't you think it might make all the difference? We all love him, don't we? Please don't let's be enemies, Doreen. Won't you come and give me a hug?'

Anne extended her arms and took a step forward. For an instant Doreen's expression crumpled and softened, like a small child's when she is suddenly overwhelmed by her own feelings, and I thought she was going to respond, but the moment passed, and a second later she was gone, slamming the door behind her.

'I feel very sorry for that family,' said Anne sadly, as I gave her a hug instead. 'Finding a new way will be so difficult . . .'

## Wednesday 20 April

Anne came downstairs this evening holding a sheet of paper and a photograph.

'Look,' she said, 'here's an old letter of Andromeda's. I don't think we've looked at this for years. It was right at the back of the bottom drawer in our room, with the photograph she sent. So sweet! Have a look.'

We first knew Andromeda Veal, who happens to be Edwin's niece, when she was a little girl of about six. She came to stay with us for a while, and, influenced very heavily by her mother and her mother's friend Gwenda, she constantly criticized me and just about everyone else, for being anti-feminist and not sufficiently committed to the socialist cause. Her favourite phrase, I seem to remember, was 'I'm afraid I don't find that very funny.'

Later, Andromeda went into hospital with a broken femur, and was in traction for some time. We became quite good friends then through letters and visits, and Andromeda actually became a Christian round about that time. She adored Anne and was deeply in love with Gerald, who lent her his personal stereo for the duration of her hospital stay, although she invariably referred to it as his 'personal problem'.

Nowadays, Andromeda lives with her stormy but reunited parents in London. The letter Anne found must have been written not long after Andromeda came out of hospital. This is what she said, exactly as she spelt it:

Dear Anne and Geruld and nice fashist, *(That's me, by the way)*

As you awl knoe, my lemur is suffishently reecoverd and nittid togetha for me to stop being an attraction and go home with mother and Gwenda, who hav temper rarilee stoppt being green and common wimmen becos the docter says I need sum comeforlessons or sumthing, so I am back in my own room exept that Gwenda says in a I deal world nobody wood own ennything but evrybody in the world wood own evrything. I ecspect shes right, but awl I knoe is

159

I cried a bit when I got back to my room that evrybody in the werld owns and Im glad the rest of the werld was out.

Mother and me bowth have secrits from Gwenda now Anne. My secrit is Lucky Lucy the dolly that you choze becos shes gott tuff nickers. You left her for me when I was asleep and horizontall. O Anne I do *luv* Lucky Lucy even if she is sosieties tool for reinforsing the subjektiv female roll. As you knoe the ownly uther dolly I ever had was a littel plastic man that Gwenda made me call Bigot and he becayme a victim of dumbestick vilence. I had to snuggle Lucky Lucy out of the hospitall and now she livs in a little cubbord in my room like Ann franc in Hampster damn. Daddy says Gwenda makes the gestarpo look like soshul werkers so I hope she dosnt find Lucky Lucy.

Mothers secrit is that daddy came to the hospital and thay got awl luvvy duvvy and she keeps glarnsing at daddys foto on the side and hes cumming to see her soon and Mothers trying too summun up the curridge to tell Gwenda enuff is enuff. O Anne I so wont to hav my mummy and daddy togetha again.

Ennyway the reeson I rearly rote was to say that my cuzzin Merle is getting marrid soon and o Anne she wonts me to be a brydesdmade and where a pritty dress and awl that. Immagin working up the I'll behind the bryde Anne eh? Acey-pacey ecsiting! Gwenda poopood in the hole idear becos she said marrige is a mail device to enshore feemale submishon and Mother pritended to agree with her but O Anne she secritlee bort my dress and took a pickture of me atchewally in it and hear it is in this letta. Daddy says Mother is week but luvvlee.

Just supose it was me who cort the bucket when the bryde throse it Anne. That wood mean its me next! Geruld isnt marrid or ingaged or enny of that is he?

Logical bonds,
     Andromeda and Lucky Lucy.

P.S. Tell Geruld if hes feeling a bit lost withowt his persunnel problem heel have to cum and get it.

Had a look at the photograph. It showed a radiant Andromeda in her bridesmaid's dress, with Mum peeping nervously out from behind her shoulder. That photo can't have been taken long before the infamous Gwenda moved out and hero daddy moved back in.

Must invite Andromeda down again some time, and see what sort of sixteen-year-old she's turned out to be.

## Thursday 21 April

Anne phoned Doreen today and tried to talk to her, but all she got was icy politeness. Glad she tried, though.

## Friday 22 April

Gerald very quiet at dinner tonight. As we finished eating, he leaned back in his chair and said, 'Any chance we could have a bit of a chat on Sunday evening?'

Anne and I froze, me with a piece of Cathedral Cheddar halfway to my mouth, she in the act of scraping scraps from one plate onto another. Knew we were both wondering the same thing – was Gerald intending to solve the mystery of his three months off work and the long walks and the occasional unexplained absences? Very slowly and casually brought my piece of cheese to its intended destination. Anne continued with her scraping, but went on absentmindedly moving her knife across the plate for a few seconds after there was nothing left to scrape. Both so anxious not to overreact that neither of us said anything at all.

Gerald said, 'Hello! Anyone out there? I know it wasn't the most dynamic of questions but I'd appreciate even the briefest of replies – if it's not too much trouble, that is.'

Anne and I immediately launched into high-pitched laughing, compensatory babbling mode. One of the things I really like about Anne is her vulnerability when it comes to anything important connected with Gerald. She's so wise and calm with everyone else, but with him it's different. I must tell her that sometime (perhaps).

Agreed to 'chat' on Sunday evening.

## Saturday 23 April

Went for a long walk over the hills with Richard today. Poor old chap finds it very difficult to communicate easily when real feelings are involved. Told me that he and Charles are getting on very well, although Charles is still adamant that the whole Christian 'thing' is not for him. Felt like crying when Richard said that he'd privately repented before the Lord for piling religious expectations on his son instead of simply loving him.

Asked how Doreen was.

Richard said she's very angry and tight-lipped. Will hardly speak to Charles, and blames just about everything on Anne and one or two other people in the church. Says he doubts if she'll continue her involvement with my support group.

'I wish,' said Richard dolefully, 'that we were like you and Anne and Gerald. You must feel so glad that Gerald's settled in his faith and everything.'

Agreed automatically, then suddenly realized that for all I'm supposed to be so open about myself I very rarely share what's troubling me *now*. I suppose that's why so many Christian speakers only ever seem to have problems in the past. Told Richard about our forthcoming 'chat' with Gerald, and how nervous we both were. He was so pleased to have something to comfort *me* about. Prayed together on a wooden seat overlooking the valley, then strolled down to a little pub I know where they do the most *excellent* pint of bitter. I know heaven is different things for different people, but settling down into the corner of a pub with a pint and a friend takes some beating.

Can't get to sleep tonight. Find myself wondering, as I used to wonder in the past, whether I would ever have been able to offer Gerald as a sacrifice, like Abraham with Isaac. Funny to think about all those times in the past when I used to apologize to God for loving Gerald more than I loved Jesus. Couldn't and can't imagine choosing between them. I tell myself I don't have that problem now that I understand God a little bit better. Not quite sure though. Wonder if Gerald knows how much I love him. Don't suppose he does. Should say these things more perhaps.

Yes, and mmmmmmmmmmmmmmmmmmmmmmmmm
mmmmmmmmmmmmmmmmmmmmmmmmmmmmmmmmm
mmmmmmmmmmmmmmmmmmmmmmmmmmmmmmmmm

## Easter Sunday 24 April

Woke up at midnight last night to find that I'd stupidly nodded off with my finger on the 'm' button of my portable word processor. Did thirty-five pages of 'm' before waking up. Deleted them and went back to sleep. Thought I'd leave a few in just to keep the record accurate. Anne says that this decision is my final qualification for long-term institutional care.

Sometimes think my word processor despises me. It says scathing things like: DO YOU REALLY WANT TO SAVE THIS?

Easter Sunday is my favourite service, I think. Anything seems possible on Easter Sunday. Come to think of it – I suppose anything's possible *because* of Easter Sunday.

Didn't want the service to end today. Didn't want the evening to come.

Tea predictably a rather tense meal this evening. Anne ate hardly anything.

'Let's leave the washing-up,' Gerald suggested as we finished, looking at me because it was my turn. 'You and Mum go through to the sitting-room and I'll bring you a coffee.'

Went down the hall to the sitting-room with Anne, feeling, for some reason, as if we were joint job-applicants who had lied in pursuit of the post for which we were about to be interviewed. All sorts of nightmare scenarios flitted through my mind as we sat neatly together on the settee. Tried to blank them off. Felt a shiver go through me as I heard him coming along the hall. Everything could change in the next five minutes.

Looked at Anne. She blew out a breath she'd been holding in for some time and said, 'Well, then.'

'Yes,' I said, 'just what I was thinking.'

Gerald fussed around with our coffee for an unnecessarily long time before sitting down in the armchair facing us. Took a few sips from a glass of something that was definitely not coffee.

I said, in what was supposed to be a joky tone, but came out like something from the darkest bits of Macbeth, 'We're not going to need one of those, then, Gerald?'

'Well, I'm not sure,' said Gerald without smiling. 'You might, actually. Do you want me to get you one?'

'Please, Gerald,' Anne was looking rather white, 'please say what it is you have to say. I'm not very good at dentists' waiting rooms.'

'Nor am I,' I said, suddenly very much not wanting to hear what Gerald had to say. 'When I was at college a little group of us who all hated the dentist got together and pledged that whenever one of us had to go to have a tooth out, at least one of the others would go with him or her to make it a bit more bearable. As far as I can remember, we called ourselves the Action Faction for Distraction from Reaction to Extraction, and we met – '

'Adrian,' said Anne.

'Yes?'

'Please be quiet.'

'Sorry.'

'Right,' said Gerald, 'here we go then.' He looked at us for a moment. 'What I have to say to you may come as a bit of a surprise. To be honest, it surprised me when – well, when it happened. Let me tell you what it isn't, just to put your minds at rest. For instance, I'm not gay.'

Anne and I fell about laughing on the sofa. Gay indeed! As if we'd ever worried about such a thing! What a hoot! In any case we have a warmly compassionate view of such things, so we'd have handled it, wouldn't we?

Breathed an inward sigh of relief. Nightmare scenario number one out of the way, thank God.

'Nor am I pregnant,' said Gerald solemnly.

Well, this *was* turning out to be a jolly session! Not pregnant – ha, ha, ha!

'Nor have I impregnated anybody else.'

Phew! That was n.s. number two disposed of. Perhaps it wouldn't be anything very alarming after all. Perhaps it was just going to be –

'I'm going to be a male stripper,' said Gerald.

Sat and stared in utter amazement. Hurriedly scanned my list of nightmare scenarios. Not a male stripper in sight.

I said, 'Gerald, I'm absolutely – '

'Adrian,' interrupted Anne, 'I think that might have been a joke, don't you?'

'Sorry, Dad,' said Gerald penitently, 'finding it a bit tricky coming to the point.' He cleared his throat. 'It's about my faith, actually.'

Found myself harking back nostalgically to those dear distant days, a few seconds ago, when I'd thought my only son was planning to make a living as a male stripper. After all, what was so very wrong with taking your clothes off in public? Found myself pleading silently with God:

'Don't let it be that Gerald doesn't believe anything any more. All those nights when he was little – you must remember how I'd creep into his bedroom when he was asleep and talk to you about him – ask you, sometimes with tears in my eyes, to look after him and keep him close to you? That was a prayer, and you answer prayer, don't you? Don't you?'

'Do you remember, Dad,' said Gerald, 'that time when Father John came to speak at the church, and said heaven would have to involve some cricket just for you?'

'Mmm.' I nodded and smiled, remembering that particular service very well indeed. It had solved a long-standing problem for me.

'Well, at coffee time afterwards I was having a bit of a chat with him, and he said, right out of the blue, "Ever thought that you might end up in the Anglican ministry?" I didn't know what to say, so I suppose I was a bit flippant. I said that, firstly, I didn't really know what the Anglican Church was, secondly, I hadn't got anything to preach, and, thirdly, God was still a complete mystery to me. He laughed and said, "In that case you precisely fulfil the normal qualifications. In fact, I'm pretty sure that, if he was here now, the bishop would ordain you on the spot." I thought it was quite funny at the time, but I certainly didn't take it very seriously.

Over the years, though – it's funny really – I've heard Father John's voice asking me that question in my mind over and over again. It's been like a sort of pointless secret that's not worth sharing with anyone else, but, then, one Sunday about a year ago, I went to this Anglican church just up the road from where I was living. I'd been there a few times before, actually, but I don't really know why. It wasn't particularly lively, and the vicar looked kind of defeated. I knew he must be feeling threatened by his congregation the first time I went there – I mean, you're supposed to begin your sermon with "Dearly beloved", aren't you, not "Ladies and gentlemen of the jury"?'

I tittered dutifully, filled with relief that my son was neither gay nor pregnant nor about to become the unscheduled male stripper. Anne didn't laugh. She clicked her tongue impatiently.

'Sorry, Mumsy,' said Gerald, 'silly joke – bit embarrassed. I was sitting in the evening service on this particular Sunday, my presence probably having lowered the average age of the congregation to about eighty-three, and I'd just been asking myself what on earth I thought I was doing there, when a sort of feeling went through me. That's the only way I can describe it – like a beam of light filling me up and passing on, but – but leaving behind a quiet sort of sureness that I was going to end up . . .'

Gerald didn't seem to be quite able to finally say the words.

'Say it, Gerald,' said Anne.

'I heard that same question again, even clearer than before – just the same words, except that this time it wasn't Father John asking, and this time I said 'Yes'. I think God was asking me to become a priest in the Anglican Church. I know one or two people would attack me with several specially sharpened chunks of Scripture for saying that, but that's their problem, I'm afraid. I don't mean that nastily, but I sure as eggs do mean it.'

Anne said, 'Of course.'

'So, over the last few months,' continued Gerald, 'I've been walking and thinking and praying and doing bits of writing for you, Dad, and just checking that I've not got carried away by my own imagination. I was sure before, but I'm even surer now. That's what I'm going to do, and I've been to see the director of thingum-mybobs and set the whole thing in motion.' He smiled at us as he's been smiling at us for twenty-four years. 'What do you think?'

Finished the bottle of not-coffee between us.

Anne and Gerald have gone to bed now. Anne seems very peaceful about Gerald's news, and I think I am, but there are one or two little worries. What will Edwin think about him going off into one of what some people describe as the 'dead limbs' of the body? What do I think? What does God think? Well, I suppose, as he's the one who suggested it, he must think it's quite a good idea. Can't imagine Gerald in a backwards collar, like my friend Vladimir. I know it's late, but I think I'll give Edwin a ring and see what he says.

### five minutes later

Edwin already knew. Says it was him who advised Gerald to go for it. Asked him if he agreed with the people who say that traditional denominations are dead limbs.

He said, 'People who mend shoes. Good night.'

## Monday 25 April

Just occurred to me that all my worry horses fell before the final fence – thank goodness. Trouble is (in my life anyway) there always seems to be another race with plenty of runners, all ready to begin, just around the corner.

## Tuesday 26 April

Very odd being at work with Glander now that he's a Christian. We're a bit uneasy with each other at the moment, trying to work out what's going to take the place of my defensive bleating and his sarcastic retorts. He's putting up with a lot of stick from some of the other blokes at work who used to enjoy hearing him put me and my faith down. Have to admit feeling a fair bit of admiration for the way he's sticking to his guns. But I still don't like him.

Anne says we should ask him to come and eat with us soon, so that we can start to make real friends.

Oh, Lord, couldn't I do something more pleasant, like turning frogs inside out and eating the squidgy bits?

Sorry – I will try.

## Wednesday 27 April

Amazing evening at our house. Started quite normally with the support group coming round for one of our usual meetings. Surprised to see that Doreen turned up after all. Didn't look very happy, and didn't say much, but she was there.

All seemed to be going well except that I was a bit worried about Leonard. Didn't say or do *anything* silly or loony during the main, business bit of the evening when we were giving some feedback on the Australian trip, and he looked very low. When coffee time came, and everyone had stopped talking for a minute, I said, 'Leonard, is there something wrong that we could help you with? You don't look very happy at all.'

Leonard usually loves being the centre of attention – that's why I waited till everyone was listening. Didn't perk up at all now, though. He said, 'Sorry I've been miserable, everybody. With giving up the booze and then Mother dying and' – glancing at Edwin – 'that not being a good enough excuse to start drinking again, I think I'm going through – ' pause, as he screwed his eyes up as if trying to remember something. Suddenly raised an index finger. 'That's it – I think I'm going through the long dark night of the haddock.'

Rather tense silence punctuated by suppressed choking sounds from one part of the room.

Edwin didn't even smile. He said seriously, 'Leonard, I think you mean "soul", don't you?'

'Oh, yes, that's right,' said Leonard mournfully. 'Well, I knew it was a fish. Anyway, that's what I'm going through. I keep crying on my own at home.'

Murmurs of concern from everyone at this plaintive confession.

'Oh, Lenny-baby, come to Glor-bags!' Gloria Marsh, who is very kind as well as being – the other things she is, was sitting beside Thynn on the sofa. Bottom lip thrust out in sympathy, she was almost crying herself. Flung her arms round him and cuddled him so closely into her chest that his head completely disappeared. Slightly distracted by this for a fleeting moment, but I really was worried about Leonard.

Richard said, with real concern in his voice, 'Leonard, have you asked the Lord to uphold you in this time of trial?'

Strange, muffled sounds floating up from the area of Gloria's bosom suggested that Leonard was doing his best to reply. When she released him he came up crimson-faced and breathless. Later, Gerald said he'd had the air of a half-drowned man anxious to be given artificial respiration so that he can get back in the water as soon as possible.

'I'm sorry,' he said, after getting his breath, 'I didn't quite catch the question. My ears were – were covered.'

'I was enquiring,' repeated Richard, 'as to whether or not you have asked the Lord to uphold you in this time of trial.'

'Yes,' said Leonard simply. 'It didn't work.'

Richard nodded, but a strangely determined expression appeared on Doreen's face. 'Leonard, the Lord always upholds his people in their time of need. Would you like me to lay hands on you and pray his blessing down upon you, as I have done in the past?'

'No, thank you, Doreen,' replied Leonard, his voice flatter and wearier than I've ever heard it before. 'It's quite hard work pretending to feel better – don't think I can manage it today. Sorry.'

Leonard wasn't being nasty. He was just too depressed to come out with anything but the truth.

Doreen went white, stood up and said to Edwin, 'This is a mockery of the Lord's work. I refuse to involve myself any further. I shall now leave.'

As Anne said later, Doreen had clearly come in order to go, as it were, and this was the trigger she had been waiting for. Edwin didn't try to stop her. He just nodded gently.

As she reached the door, Doreen stopped, and in a voice so brittle that it almost broke, she said, 'Richard, are you coming?'

We all wanted to be somewhere else at that moment. Richard, who was sitting with his face in his hands, didn't move. He replied, with a pathetic attempt to keep his voice normal, 'Er, no, you go ahead, dear, I'll follow on a little later.'

She looked at him for just a moment, and then went. Something important had happened.

Nobody spoke for a while, then Edwin said, as if to himself, 'As Father John used to tell us, there's never anything but trouble when you allow vulgar truth to creep into the Church. Let's get back to business.'

He turned to Leonard.

'Look, Leonard, forget for the moment what anyone else says. If you want to, and *only* if you want to, just tell us exactly how you feel. Never mind what you're *supposed* to think or feel – that's not important. And we'll just listen, okay? Or if you prefer, we won't say another word about it now – we'll talk about something else, and you and I can have a chat later. It's up to you.'

Gloria held Leonard's left hand tightly in both of hers and smiled encouragingly at him.

'Well,' said Leonard, 'it's just that – ' He looked round at us all and sighed dismally. 'I don't think I've ever really believed any of it – all the God things, I mean. Not like the rest of you, anyway. Adrian gets all excited about it when he's talking to lots of people, even if he is different in real life.' Tried to avoid blushing by an act of the will. 'But I don't. And I haven't heard God speak to me like he speaks to Richard and – and Doreen all the time. Why does he always say lots of things to them and never anything to me?'

Not a complaint, just a question.

(Couldn't help remembering the conversation Anne and Gerald and I had with Charles in our kitchen. How many others are there, for goodness sake?)

Edwin shook his head slowly. 'Well, I'd have to line up with you on that one, Leonard,' he said quietly, 'I'm afraid God doesn't have an awful lot of specific things to say to me either. Mind you, I'm probably not very good at listening . . .'

'But you do believe in him, don't you?' said Leonard, a trace of alarm sounding in his voice. Some walls, after all, are supporting ones.

'Oh, yes,' answered Edwin, his voice barely a whisper, but filled, as Anne put it so well afterwards, with the warmth and passion of a man who is deeply in love. 'I do believe in him – I always have done. I belong to him.'

'I don't think I belong to anything, really,' said Leonard dolefully. 'I'm not very good at the things you all are.' There was a short silence, then he frowned suddenly, and the very essence of his deepest trouble was etched into the lines of that dark expression. 'I think he doesn't want me because I'm silly.'

Leonard's eyes filled with tears and so did most of ours.

At this moment, Stephanie Widgeon, who had contributed virtually nothing to the conversation all evening, leaned towards the sofa and said, 'Leonard, dear, I know that we have been friends for only a very short time, but I would like to pass on to you something that has been a great comfort to me.'

'Oh, no,' I muttered under my breath, 'please don't say we're getting the bloody Church-is-not-the-building bit now – *surely* not now! Stop her, Edwin!'

But he didn't – this man who never hears from God didn't stop her.

'You see,' went on Stephanie, her eyes sparkling, 'the Church is not just a building – it's actually the people inside who are the Church. Have you ever heard that idea before, Leonard?'

'Yes,' said Leonard, his truth-telling mechanism still very much in operation, 'from you – every time I see you. And I never have understood what you mean. The Church is a building, usually a big grey one made of stone, and the people who go to it aren't churches, they're people.'

'Ah, yes,' trilled Stephanie, undaunted, 'but that is in a material sense. I am speaking spiritually.'

She sat back and beamed at us all, clearly convinced once again that she had introduced the group to an entirely novel concept. I decided we'd had enough of this.

I said, 'Edwin, don't you think this is the wrong time for this sort of – '

He put up a hand to stop me (very unusual for Edwin to stop

anyone in mid-sentence). 'No, Adrian, I think that what Stephanie has said is the most important thing of all for Leonard to hear.'

Stephanie's beam became a positive beacon.

'You see, Leonard,' continued Edwin gently, 'Stephanie is absolutely right when she says that the *real* Church – not the building, but the people who have to be Jesus in the world until he comes back – is, well, it's just us. If there was *only* you and I left, then we would be the Church – us two, Edwin Burlesford and Leonard Thynn, the body of Jesus on earth. And neither of us would be more important than the other because the Bible says that all the parts are equal and that we belong to each other. Do you understand that?'

Leonard nodded his head vigorously and said, 'No, not really.'

Edwin said, 'Anne, do you have a candle we could use, please?'

A couple of minutes later our only light source was the flickering flame of a white, household candle, balanced in a saucer on the coffee table in the middle of the room. Edwin asked us to all hold hands and sit in silence for a moment. When he spoke his voice was very clear and deliberate.

'Leonard, I am an alcoholic, managing by the skin of my teeth to avoid having a drink each day. In the past I have been arrested on the street, and sometimes ridiculed by people who hear me claim to be a Christian when they know me only as a drunk. Nobody really knows how hard I have to fight to live without alcohol.'

Even in the dim light thrown by the candle it was easy to make out the expression of astonishment on Leonard's face. 'But, that's exactly what I – you never told me that you were a . . .' Realization dawned. 'You mean that you . . .'

'I am very proud,' said Edwin softly, 'to own and share the good and the bad, the sense and the silliness in you, Leonard, my dear brother. I want you to know that your fights and victories are my fights and victories. Your failures are my failures. I hope that you can share the good and the bad in me as well – much more bad than you think, I'm afraid. But I do believe in God – this week anyway – so, I tell you what, since we are brothers, and parts of the same body, I'll hold your unbelief and you can hold my faith.' He smiled. 'That'll confuse God so much that he'll put up with both of us. I think that's the kind of confusion he likes. Jesus so wanted us to love each other. Tell me, Leonard, do you believe in the hands that are touching yours at this moment?'

'Yes,' said Leonard, 'they're real people.'

'That's right, and these real people are parts of Jesus, so when you hold their hands you are actually holding hands with God. Whatever one of us lacks, all of us lack. Whatever one of us owns, all of us share.'

Leonard looked slowly from Gloria on his left to Anne on his right and smiled his first watery little smile of the evening.

Edwin glanced around the group. 'You know, I feel more lucky than I can say to be serving as an elder. When I look at just this little group here I realize how rich I am. Stephanie has shared that little piece of truth with us – more than once, it's true, but what a great truth, and so right for what's happening here tonight; Leonard, lovable and quite unique; dear Anne, so warm and wise; Gloria, full of compassion and need; Gerald, who has brightened my day on many, many occasions, and is now being called by God to a very specific task; Richard and Doreen, troubled at present, but loyal friends in the past, anxious to serve God – too anxious sometimes, perhaps, and Adrian, who undervalues all his strengths and has made the world a gift of his weaknesses. I don't want to sound too soppy, but it's such a pleasure to know that all those qualities are mine as well as yours. As for the more negative things – well, we share all those as well, and because of that we do need to take turns being Jesus for each other, don't you think? I certainly need all of you to do that for me.'

We sat quietly looking at the flame for quite a long time after that.

I don't think I shall go on writing a diary after this, but there's one last thing I want to put down. It's what I tried to say to Anne just now before she went to sleep.

I tried to say that there are days when I feel very worried and confused about the Church – a little frightened even at times. But, as we sat in the darkness of our sitting-room this evening, with that tiny light shining in the middle of our group, I knew in the very heart of my heart that the Church – Stephanie's real Church – will be all right in the end. And it will be all right because there will always be just a few people like Edwin around in every generation – people who, when the tongues have stopped, and the prophecies have ended, and the kangaroo-hopping has come to a standstill, and the religious posing and posturing fools nobody any more, will still be ready and willing to genuinely share the burdens of the little people who are close to them, committed to the staggering eternal truth that we are one body because we all partake of the one bread.

And I guess they'll be like that because they want, if only in some small way, to be like their master and friend, who long ago hung on a cross, not ashamed at all to be as broken and as silly as Leonard Thynn, and Adrian Plass, and Everett Glander and the others in my church, and the whole of the rest of the world, because he loved us.

## Thursday 28 April

One last thing.

Said to Gerald today, 'It's just occurred to me that you used to produce a constant stream of anagrams. What happened to all that misdirected creative energy?'

He smiled as he went out of the room and said, 'Oh, I just grew out of it, I suppose.'

Five minutes later he reappeared with a very serious expression on his face, and a piece of paper in his hand, and said, 'Dad, something quite important's come up.'

'Yes,' I said, 'what?'

'Did you know,' replied Gerald, 'that TORONTO BLESSING is an anagram of something an obedient angel probably said to his squadron leader immediately after launching the new wave?'

'No, I didn't know that. What did he say?'

'He said, "LO, GRIN BOOST SENT!"'

## Friday 29 April

One absolutely, definitely last thing.

Today I finally solved a problem that's troubled me for years. I have never received anything like a satisfactory answer to the following question:

WHY DID LEONARD THYNN BORROW OUR CAT?

Everywhere I go, people who've read my first book want to know why Leonard came round one day to ask us to loan him the cat. Today I decided to finally get the truth out of him. Sat him down at the kitchen table and put it to him straight.

'Leonard, do you remember when you borrowed our cat?'

Troubled look. 'Yes.'

'Why did you?'

'The truth?'

'Yes, the truth.'

'Well, I'd never had an animal, and – '

'The truth, Leonard!'

'The truth?'

'The truth.'

'I had this tape recorder and – '

'Leonard!'

Pause – very small voice, 'Ran out of excuses for coming round, Adrian . . .'

Must look up 'cleistogamic' in the dictionary.

We want to hear from you. Please send your comments about this book to us in care of zreview@zondervan.com. Thank you.

GRAND RAPIDS, MICHIGAN 49530 USA

WWW.ZONDERVAN.COM